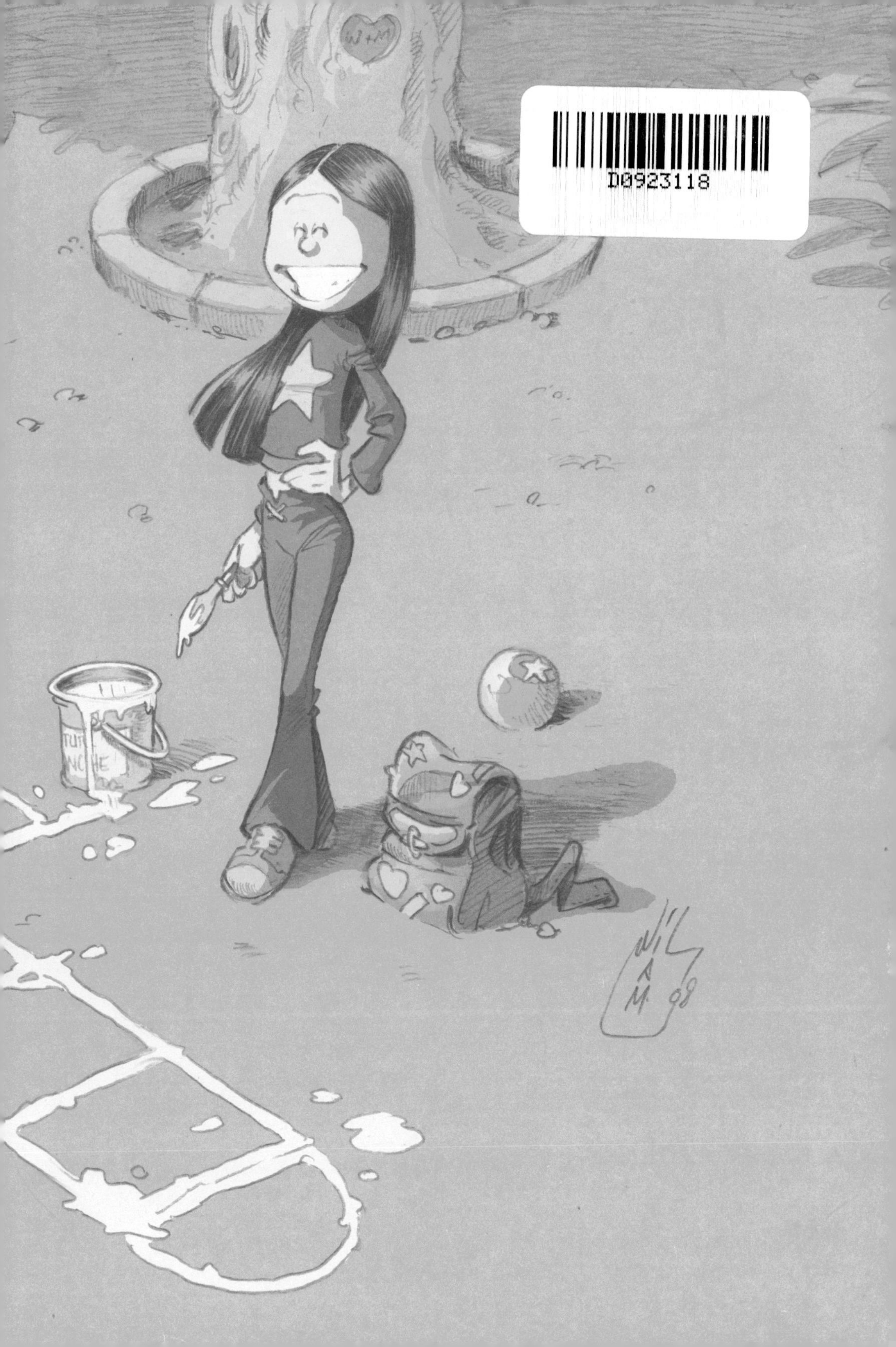

The Sisters

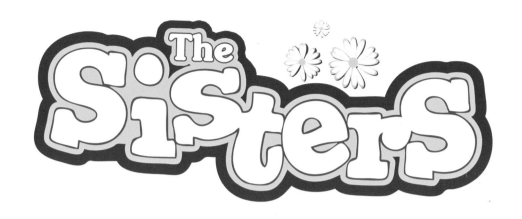

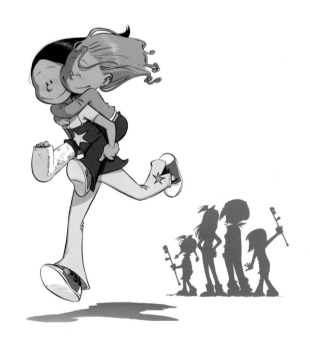

PAPERCUTZ

MORE GREAT GRAPHIC NOVEL SERIES AVAILABLE FROM PAPERCUTZ

THE SMURFS #21

MINNIE & DAISY #1

DISNEY FAIRIES #18

THE GARFIELD SHOW #6

BARBIE #1

TROLLS #1

GERONIMO STILTON #17

THEA STILTON #6

NANCY DREW DIARIES #7

BARBIE PUPPY PARTY

THE LUNCH WITCH #1

SCARLETT

ANNE OF GREEN BAGELS #1

THE RED SHOES

FUZZY BASEBALL

THE SISTERS #1

THE SISTERS #2

THE SISTERS #3

THE SISTERS #4

SUPER SISTERS

3: "Honestly, I Love My Sister"

Art and colors
William

Story
Cazenove & William

PAPERCUTZ

New York

To my grandparents: Lucette and André!

Thank you again, Christophe (the "joke incubator"); and to Olivier, for your trust.

Bravo, Arno, "ABI" for your "cast horse" joke and bravo, Noémie, for your "cast hold-all" joke.

A short note from Marine ("Maureen"): "Hey there, to all my friends, who I love so much, even if they're not all in my daddy's graphic novel."

A short note from Wendy: "I don't believe it)O_0...Now she's even crashing the acknowledgements page... ≩tsk, tsk, tsk...≨ What a goofball. But I love that little brat anyway ^ ^ !"

Don't copy any of the stunts shown in this graphic novel at home. The characters on these pages are overtrained and semi-pros at controlled falls ^ ^ !

—William

THE SISTERS #3 "Honestly, I Love My Sister"
Les Sisters [The Sisters] by Cazenove and William
© 2010, 2011 Bamboo Édition
Sisters, characters and related indicia are copyright, trademark and exclusive license of Bamboo Édition. English translation and all other editorial material © 2017 by Papercutz
All rights reserved.

Story by Christophe Cazenove and William Maury
Art and color by William
Cover by William
Translation by Nanette McGuinness
Lettering by Wilson Ramos Jr.

For information address:
Bamboo Édition –116, rue des Jonchères – BP 3, 71012 CHARNAY-lès-MÂCON cedex FRANCE
bamboo@bamboo.fr – www.bamboo.fr

Papercutz books may be purchased for business or promotional use. For information on bulk purchases please contact Macmilan Corporate and Premium Sales Department at (800) 221-7945 x5442

Production — Dawn K. Guzzo
Editor — Robert V. Conte
Assistant Managing Editor — Jeff Whitman
Jim Salicrup
Editor-in-Chief

ISBN: 978-1-62991-645-3 Paperback Edition
ISBN: 978-1-62991-646-0 Hardcover Edition

Printed in China
August 2017

Distributed by Macmillan
First Papercutz Printing

WHAT DID I TELL YOU, *MAUREEN*? LOOKS LIKE MORE *SPRING CLEANING* AND *VACUUMING* FOR US...

OH, NOOOO, *WENDY*-- HOUSEWORK MAKES ME BREAK OUT IN *HORROR-HIVES*!

YOU KNOW WHAT? THIS TIME, LET'S TRICK *MOM* AND *DAD*!

HA! THAT'S A GOOD IDEA!

OKAY, YOU'LL GO DOWN THE STAIRS AT *TOP SPEED*...

...AND I'LL CHASE AFTER YOU, *SCREAMING*...

...AS IF YOU'D BEEN GOING THROUGH MY ROOM... *THE USUAL DRILL*...

...THEN WE'LL QUICKLY CROSS THE LIVING ROOM AND *GET OUT OF THE HOUSE* BEFORE THEY CAN NAB US!

WOW... SUPER COOL PLAN!

OKAY, LET'S GO!

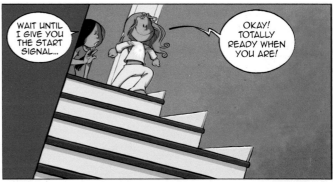

WAIT UNTIL I GIVE YOU THE START SIGNAL...

OKAY! TOTALLY READY WHEN YOU ARE!

3...2...1... — GO!

GERONIMO!

AH, MAUREEN! YOU'RE JUST *IN TIME*. HERE, GRAB THE VACUUM CLEANER AND HELP US FOR A WHILE...

OH, NOOOO...UM, WENDYYY?

HEE-HEE! IT'S SO AWESOME BEING THE *OLDEST*!

CAZENOVE & WILLIAM

HURRY UP, MAUREEN. WE CAN'T GO OUT WITH OUR FRIENDS IF THERE'S A SINGLE SPECK OF DUST LEFT IN OUR ROOMS.

PSSSS

YEAH... *PFFFFF* I HATE CHORES...

RUB RUB

SLIPPPP...

HA-HA! SLIDING'S *GREAT*, ISN'T IT?

WAIT, I'LL ADD ANOTHER LAYER OF FOAM!

WATCH ME SKATE!

SLLLLIIIIIDE...

YOUR TURN, WENDY!

THAT'S SO *FUN*!

CHECK THIS OUT--ISN'T IT AWESOME?!

SLIIIIDE...

DUST SPRAY

HA-HA! I'M DOING IT 20 TIMES *BETTER* THAN YOU!

BONK

DING A-DING

DONG

UMM, GO ON WITHOUT US. WE HAVE A LOT OF CLEANING UP TO DO!

PLUS SKATING IS *NOT* REALLY OUR THING...

?

CAZENOVE & WILLIAM

DEAR DIARY: YOU KNOW, IF I HAD TO CHOOSE, THERE'S ONE OF MAUREEN'S FLAWS THAT SERIOUSLY GETS ON MY NERVES...

...SHE'S EXTREMELY NOISY!

RINNNGGGINGGG

I'LL GEEETTTT IT!

WHETHER SHE'S WATCHING HANNAH MATTRESS ON TV...

HA-HA-HA! MILEY CITRUS'S FACE!

...GULPING DOWN HER CHEESE, APRICOT AND BANANA SANDWICH...

EAT 5 PIECES OF FRUIT AND 5 VEGETABLES EVERY DAAAAY...

...DOING THE SHOPPING...

I PUSH THE CART SO I'M THE ONE WHO GETS TO CHOOSE THE ICE CREAM!

I GET TO! I GET TO!

I GET TO!

UH, MOM, CAN WE LOSE HER IN ONE OF THE AISLES?

...CHARGING DOWN THE STAIRS WEARING SOCKS AND SCREAMING THE WHOLE TIME...

GERONIIMOOOOOOOO...

BANGADANG

WELL, WHAT DO YOU KNOW? SHE'S ONLY QUIET WHEN SHE HURTS HERSELF!

BOO-HOO-HOOO

OH, WELL... IT WAS TOO GOOD TO BE TRUE!

7

CAZENOVE & WILLIAM

HOLY COW-- THAT WAS A *CLOSE CALL!*

GOO-GOO-GA-GA!

CATCH

DIDI

DIDI'S GOING TO TEACH YOU TO *WALK.*

YOU HAVE TO PLACE ONE FOOT FIRST, THEN THE OTHER.

GAA-GOO?

NOT BOTH OF THEM AT THE SAME TIME.

AH-NAH-NAH

AND YOU LOOK STRAIGHT AHEAD...

GA-GOOPEE!

GREAT, *MAUREEEN...* YOU'RE DOING REALLY WELL!

CLAP CLAP CLAP

GZZZ...

GOOPEE!

YIPPEE!

COME ON, *WENDY,* LET'S DO ANOTHER ONE. I FEEL LIKE I'M GETTING BETTER.

MY LIFE'S AN *ENDLESS CYCLE!*

8

CAZENOVE & WILLIAM

MAUREEN, I'M HERE!

AND I'M HERE, TOO!

YOU'D NEVER KNOW IT, BUT IT'S *TOTALLY AWESOME* TO HAVE A LEG IN A CAST...

I'M YOUR *SERVANT.*

FOR STARTERS, IT'S *MAID-SERVANT!*

I'LL CARRY YOUR BOOK BAG.

POOH, YOU HAVE TROUBLE CARRYING YOUR OWN!

MY FRIENDS *LULU* AND *NAT* ARE SUPER SWEET TO ME...

MY DADDY WILL DRIVE US TO SCHOOL.

AFTER YOU, MY DEAREST FRIEND...

WE NEED TO PROP UP YOUR LEG NICELY ON THIS PILLOW.

THANKS!

LEAN ON ME, IF YOU'D LIKE.

ME TOO, *ALWAYS!*

YOU KNOW, I'LL *ALWAYS* BE HERE FOR YOU.

IT'S NICE TO KNOW YOU'VE GOT FRIENDS WHO'RE ALWAYS THERE FOR YOU...

SO... WHO'D LIKE TO ANSWER THE QUESTION?

MAUREEN?!

SO, MAUREEN, I'M LISTENING. DO YOU KNOW THE ANSWER?!

WELL, FRIENDS WHO'RE *ALMOST* ALWAYS THERE FOR YOU...

CAZENOVE & WILLIAM

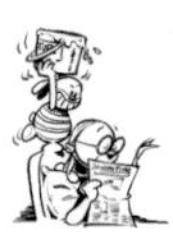

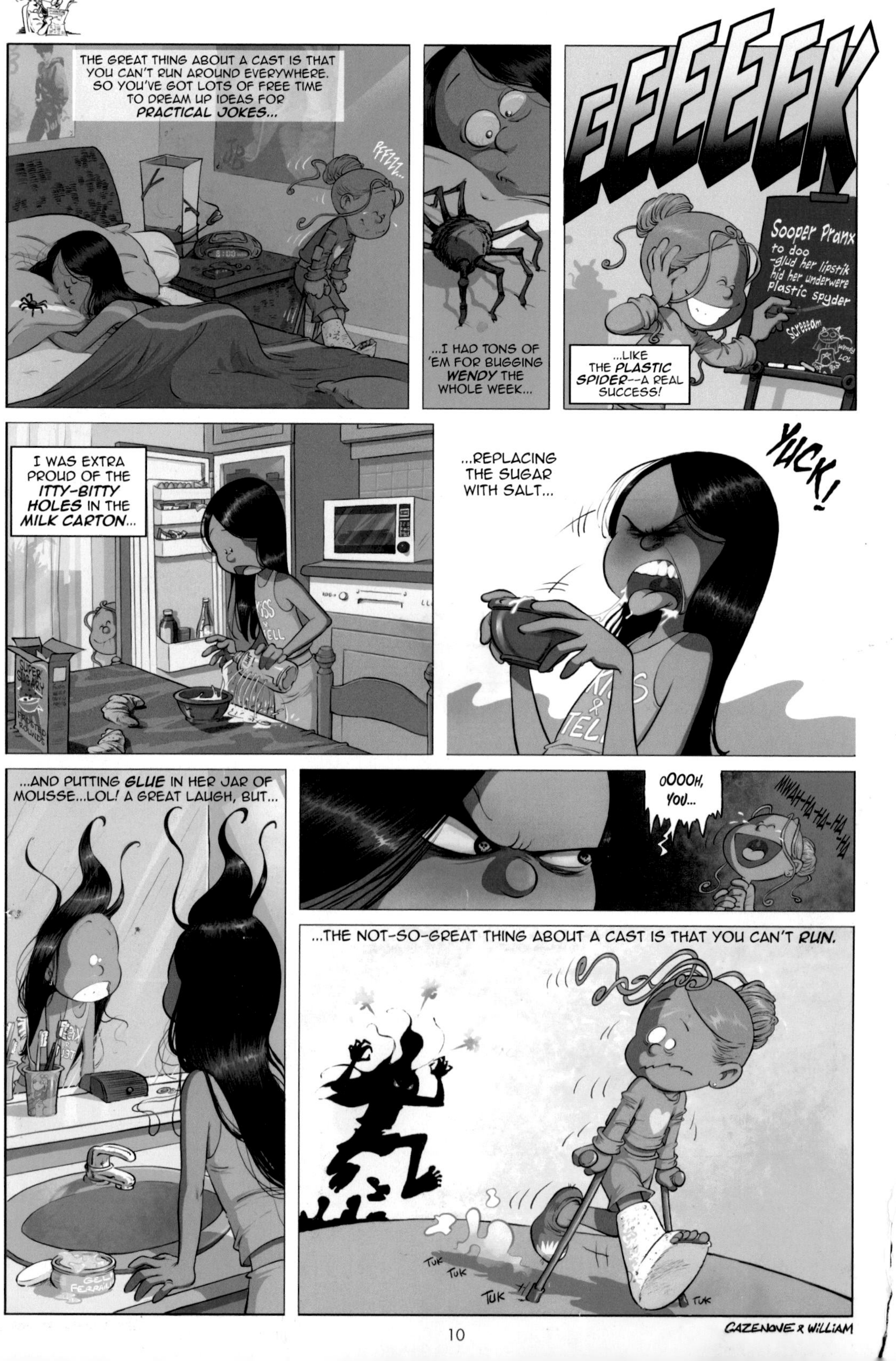

THE GREAT THING ABOUT A CAST IS THAT YOU CAN'T RUN AROUND EVERYWHERE. SO YOU'VE GOT LOTS OF FREE TIME TO DREAM UP IDEAS FOR PRACTICAL JOKES...
PFFZZZ...
...I HAD TONS OF 'EM FOR BUGGING WENDY THE WHOLE WEEK...
EEEEEK
Sooper Pranx
to doo
-glud her lipstik
hid her underwere
plastic spyder
Screeeam
...LIKE THE PLASTIC SPIDER--A REAL SUCCESS!
I WAS EXTRA PROUD OF THE ITTY-BITTY HOLES IN THE MILK CARTON...
...REPLACING THE SUGAR WITH SALT...
YUCK!
...AND PUTTING GLUE IN HER JAR OF MOUSSE...LOL! A GREAT LAUGH, BUT...
OOOOH, YOU...
MWAH-HA-HA-HA-HA
...THE NOT-SO-GREAT THING ABOUT A CAST IS THAT YOU CAN'T RUN.
TUK
TUK
TUK
TUK

CAZENOVE & WILLIAM

KNOCK-KNOCK! *ROOM SERVICE!*

KNOCK KNOCK

OKAY?

KNOCK

TOAST WITH *EMMIE'S* JAM AND *MOM'S* DIET SODA.

I'VE ALSO PEELED SOME MANDARIN ORANGES FOR YOU.

I'LL FLUFF THE PILLOWS A BIT SO THEY'RE MORE COMFORTABLE.

THEEERE...

PUFF

PUFF PUFF

HERE YOU GO. I'M LENDING YOU MY MP3 PLAYER...

...AND MY NINTENDOX, TOO. IT'S GOT A NEW GAME THAT *AUDREY* PUT IN IT.

AND ABOVE ALL...

....DON'T FORGET THE MOST IMPORTANT THING!

OKAY, I'M GOING NOW BUT WILL BE NEAR THE DOOR IF YOU NEED ANYTHING ELSE. BYE-BYE!

WOW! MAUREEN'S *A SUPER SISTER--*

--YOU'RE SO *LUCKY!*

≥PFFF...≤ YEAH, SURE. LOOK AT WHAT SHE WROTE ON THE CAST...

UMM, IT LOOKS LIKE... *MATH?*

YUP... IT'S HER *BILL!*

C.CAZENOVE & WILLIAM

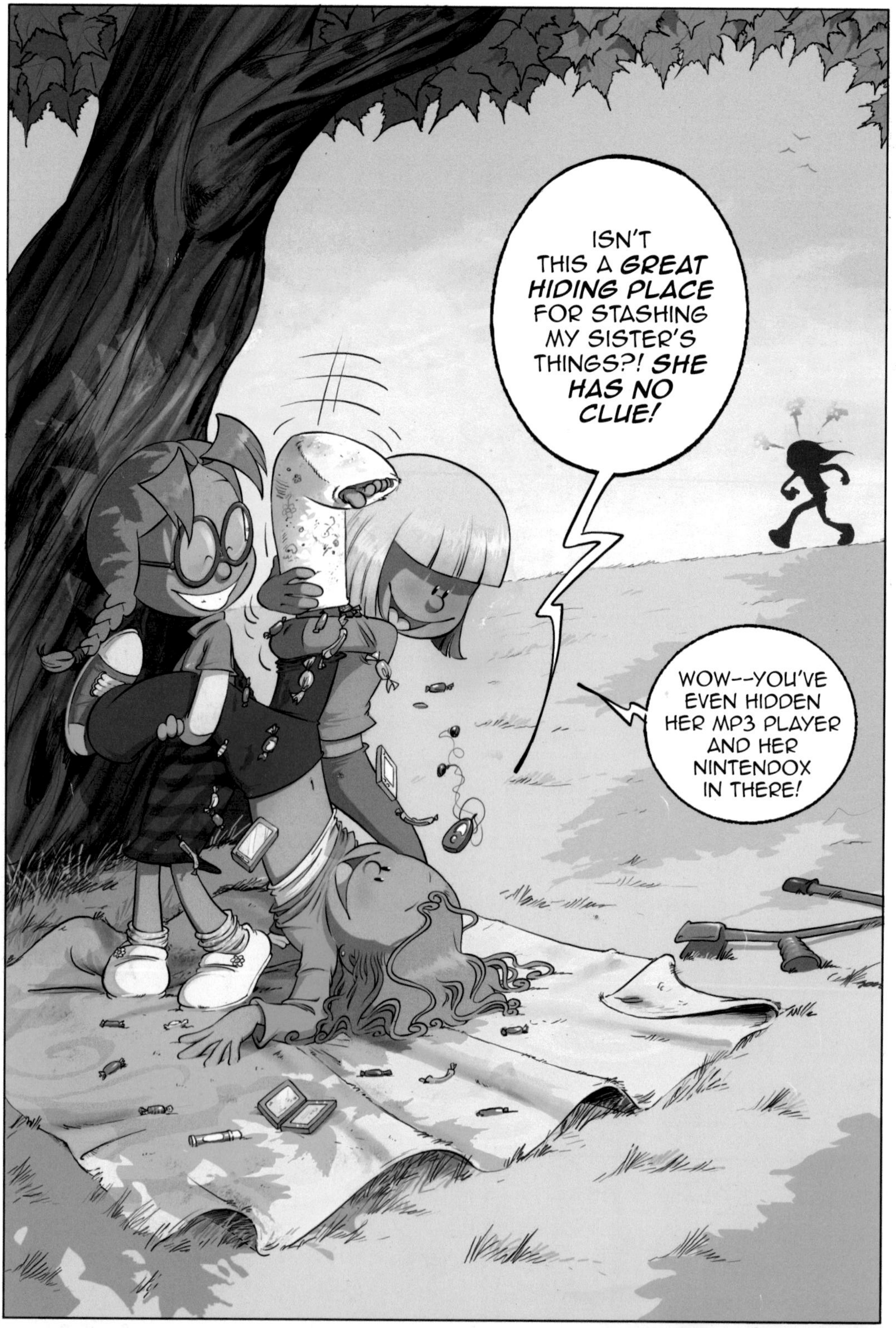
ISN'T THIS A GREAT HIDING PLACE FOR STASHING MY SISTER'S THINGS?! SHE HAS NO CLUE!
WOW--YOU'VE EVEN HIDDEN HER MP3 PLAYER AND HER NINTENDOX IN THERE!
CAZENOVE & WILLIAM

WHERE'RE WE GOING, WENDY?

CLIMB ON, CURIOUS KID!

BUT... MY CRUTCHES?

DON'T WORRY, MAUREEN. WE'LL MANAGE!

PANT PANT

PHEW PHEW

HEE-HEE-HEE

PHEW
PHEW
PANT
PANT

HUFF WE PANT ARE PUFF HERE...

THERE, DID WHEEZE YOU LIKE THE RIDE?

UMM, WELL...

GOOD. I'VE GOT SOMETHING IMPORTANT TO DO, SO I'LL LEAVE YOU HERE...

— BYE-BYE!

WOW WHEEZE HA-HA-HA... PANT HI, GIRLS...

AH, ARE WE GOING TO BE ABLE TO WATCH THAT NEW MOVIE ON MY LAPTOP?

DEFINITELY! WE'LL BE LEFT IN PEACE...

IT'LL TAKE HER AN HOUR-AND-A-HALF TO GET BACK HOME ON ONE LEG!

CAZENOVE & WILLIAM

THE HORSE IS A LARGE HERBIVOROUS, HOOFED MAMMAL THAT BELONGS TO ONE OF THE SEVEN SPECIES IN THE EQUINE FAMILY...

WHY DO YOU LOOK SO DOWN IN THE MOUTH, MAUREEN? YOU USUALLY LIKE SHOWS ABOUT HORSES!

YEAH, BUT WITH THIS CAST I WON'T BE RIDING A HORSE FOR A WHILE.

...THE MULE, THE RESULT OF CROSSING A DONKEY WITH A MARE, IS WELL KNOWN FOR ITS STRONG PERSONALITY...

I'VE GOT A GREAT IDEA! I'LL BE BACK... DON'T MOVE A MUSCLE!

RATS! I WAS ABOUT TO RUN OFF...

BONK

VZZZ GLOP

TAP

FITCH

?

HERE WE GO!

I'M COMING! I'M COMING!

AH, BUT...

...NO...

NO... WENDY!

WAIT!

BUT YES!

YOUR THINGIE IS TOTALLY LAME!

¿GRRR...¿ MAUREEN, YOU'RE NEVER HAPPY!

GO ON AND SULK THEN--THAT'S A COOL HOBBYHORSE!

HAS ANYONE SEEN THE STRAP FOR MY PURSE?

ABi, CAZENOVE & WiLLiAM

≈SIGH≈

HEY! WHAT'S WITH THE GLOOMY MUG?

DADDY'S GOING TO TAKE ME TO THE HOSPITAL SO THEY CAN TAKE OFF MY CAST.

LOL! YOU KNOW YOU RARELY GET TO KEEP THAT KIND OF THING FOR LIFE.

OH, HA-HA. DID YOU *SWALLOW A CLOWN* THIS MORNING?

DO YOU THINK THEY'LL HAVE TO BREAK IT?

OF COURSE! IT'S NOT A SOCK, YOU KNOW.

BUT LOOOK HOW PREEETTY IT IS... ALL MY FRIENDS DREW ON IT. AND ALSO *DADDY* AND *MOMMY* AND *YOU* AND EVEN *DARWIN.*

WHATEVS

UNLESS...

YAY. I HAVE A GREAT IDEA! HEE-HEE!

WHERE'RE YOU GOING? YOU KNOW DAD DOESN'T LIKE YOU HANGING OUT IN HIS OFFICE.

BUT I JUST WANT TO SCAN THE DRAWINGS!

LOL! A CAST FOR *YOUR BRAIN* IS WHAT YOU NEED...!

15

CAZENOVE & WILLIAM

I'M NOT HAPPY AT ALL, *WENDY!*

YEAH, NOT HAPPY AT ALL!

IT'S PAST TIME FOR YOU TO SETTLE DOWN AND FLY RIGHT.

YEAH, GET DOW AND FLY A KITE.

NEXT TIME, YOU'LL THINK TWICE BEFORE YOU MISBEHAVE.

YEAH, MAYBE EVEN THREE TIMES.

YOU UNDERSTAND THAT I MUST PUT MY FOOT DOWN.

YEAH, BUT I HAVE TO PUT MY FEET UP.

YOU'LL SET THE TABLE EVERY DAY FOR A MONTH!

UM..*MOM*... WOULDN'T YOU RATHER FIND *ANOTHER* PUNISHMENT?

WHAT? NO! WILL THAT BRAT SHUT HER TRAP?!

WAM

TAKE SOMETHING AWAY FROM HER. HER TELEPHONE OR NINTENDOX. SOMETHING LIKE THAT, YOU KNOW?!

HOW DO YOU EXPECT MY *PANDY* TO SET THE TABLE?

OH, COME ON, FIND ANOTHER PUNISHMENT. *PLEEEZE...?*

NO MATTER WHAT, WHEN *MAUREEN'S* IN TROUBLE, SHE SHARES THE PUNISHMENT WITH HER *STUFFED ANIMALS!*

CAZENOVE & WILLIAM

WHAT CAN YOU DO? I'M TELLING YOU, SAMMIE...

IT'S A CURSE!

I HUNG OUT AFTER SCHOOL INSTEAD OF DOING MY HOMEWORK. MY PC WAS TAKEN AWAY...

I LET SOME CURSE WORDS FLY AND MY PHONE WAS TAKEN AWAY...

I LEFT MY ROOM A MESS FOR A WEEK. MY NINTENDOX WAS TAKEN AWAY...

I BROUGHT HOME A TON OF BAD GRADES AND GOT GROUNDED...

...AND MY ALLOWANCE WAS TAKEN AWAY FOR... *ACTING OUT* AGAINST *MAUREEN*.

I *SWEAR* TO YOU, I'VE REALLY TRIED *EVERYTHING*...

...BUT NOT *ONCE* HAS MY SISTER BEEN TAKEN AWAY!

CAZENOVE & WILLIAM

WENDY, WENDY, WENDY! WANT TO KNOW SOMETHING CRAZY?

— NO!

COME OOOON...YESSSS, YOU DO...IT'S SO AWESOOOOME!

YOU KNOW HOW YESTERDAY, MOM DIDN'T WANT TO BUY ME THOSE CHOCOLATE SHOES...? AND, WELL, DO YOU KNOW WHAT I DID?

YOU HOWLED LIKED A CAR ALARM. NO NEWS THERE!

NOPE, NOPE. YOU LOSE.

I JUST CLICKED MY HEELS AND CLAPPED MY HANDS TOGETHER HARD...

...LIKE THIS!

WHATEVS!

TSK..!!

THUMP THUMP

THUMP

AND I GOT MY CHOCOLATE SHOES! HA-HA!

AND LATER, WHEN I GOT JAM ON DADDY'S DRAWINGS...

...SAME THING... HE DIDN'T SEE ANYTHING!

IT'S MAGIC! I HAVE A SPELL FOR WHEN I'M GOING TO HAVE BAD LUCK!

YAHOOO!

BAD LUCK!

I'M MAGICALLLL! NA-NA-NA-NA-NNNNNA!

SO TELL ME, DIDN'T YOU HAVE A POEM TO LEARN?

THE POEM!

SOOOO...DID YOU LEARN THAT POEM, MAUREEN?

UH-UMM...ANY SECOND NOW, MA'AM...

Monday, May 29
Poetry

PAT

PAT

PAT

TUNK

TUNK
TUNK
TUNK

18

CAZENOVE x WILLIAM

I SWEAR, NAT. MY MOTHER'S FRIEND'S GOT AN ALLERGY THAT'S TOTALLY NUTSO...

ABOVE ALL, SHE CAN'T *EAT* SHRIMP...

BUT...

...IF SHE DOES, SHE *SWEATS LIKE A SPONGE*...

EXACTLY SO, MADAM. THERE ARE, INDEED, *GROUND SHRIMP* IN THE SHRIMP CREAM.

AND *LULU* ALSO HAS ALLERGIES...

LOUISE?! NO WAYYYY!

YES, WAY. EXCEPT SHE *ITCHES ALL OVER* AS SOON AS SHE SEES A *DAISY*...

EVEN SO, THERE'S *NOTHING NICER* THAN GIVING SOMEONE A DAISY.

AND MY *AUNTIE COCO* TURNS ALL *RED* WHEN SHE GETS *STUNG BY A MOSQUITO*...

I THINK THE MOSQUITO TORCH IS EMPTY.

NO, YOU THINK?

AND IF YOU LOOK OVER THERE, THERE'S *MY SISTER* WHO'S *SWEATY* AND *TURNING BRIGHT RED ALL OVER!*

OH, JEEZ... YOU'RE RIGHT--SHE LOOKS LIKE A *TOMATO!*

WENDY, DON'T STAY THERE. YOU MUST BE ALLERGIC TO *MASON!*

CLEARLY. YOU'VE GOT ALL THE SIMPLETONS!

CAZENOVE & WILLIAM

YOU'D NEVER KNOW IT, BUT *WENDY* IS TOTALLY *OCD*...

♪ BABY BABY BABY OOOH

OH, NOT WAY! MY *CDs* GO BACK INTO THEIR CASE AND PUT THAT DOWN BEFORE IT *BREAKS!*

♪ BABY BABY OOH

TOTALLY OCD. AT BREAKFAST, TOO...

SMACK

YUM CRACK

YUCK! KEEP YOUR CRUMBS ON YOUR SIDE ALREADY!

SHE HAS A FIT WHEN I TOUCH HER THINGS...

I KNEW IT! YOU *NEVER* PUT THE CAPS BACK ON MY MARKERS... THEY'RE ALL GOING TO DRY OUT! ⨕GRRR...⨕ DIMWIT!

SHE EVEN BLOWS A FUSE WHEN I PLAY WITH MY TOYS...

THIS IS A FAMILY ROOM, NOT A *ZOO!*

HEEEYYY... YOU HURT *FAIRYZILLA...*

— TORTURER!

STILL...

...THERE'RE TIMES SHE'S NOT OCD AT ALL!

HURRY, HURRY-- MASON'S INVITED ME TO THE MOVIEEEES...

YEAH, WELL, DON'T COUNT ON *ME* TO CLEAN UP *YOUR* THINGS!

OCD: OBSESSIVE-COMPULSIVE DISORDER, IS A MENTAL DISORDER THAT WENDY DOES *NOT* HAVE. IT'S A SERIOUS PROBLEM, NOT TO BE TAKE LIGHTLY. MAUREEN DOESN'T UNDERSTAND THAT, BUT NOW YOU *DO!*

CAZENOVE & WILLIAM

COME ON, *WENDY*, TELL ME, TELL ME, TELL ME...

PRETTY PLEASE, PRETTY PLEASE, PRETTY PLEASE...

GRRR LEAVE ME ALONE, YOU GLUE STICK!

BESIDES, IT'S NONE OF YOUR BEESWAX FOR STARTERS!

PRETTY PLEASE, WENDY...

...I REALLY WANT TO KNOW WHAT IT MEANS TO BE IN LOVE.

HMMPH OKAY, BUT KEEP IT TO YOURSELF.

CROSS YOUR HEART AND HOPE TO DIE, STICK A NEEDLE IN YOUR EYE!

PINKY SWEAR. I WON'T SAY A THING!

PTOOEY

THE THING IS THAT *MASON* AND I ARE *INTENSELY CLOSE*...

...BUT IT STAYS *PLATONIC*, YOU KNOW. YOU CAN'T IMAGINE THIS...

...BUT WE'RE MADE FOR EACH OTHER.

A SIMPLE GLANCE GIVES BIRTH TO ROMANTIC FIREWORKS...

...BUT OUR RELATIONSHIP IS EVER-CHANGING, PRETTY MUCH.

IT'S WILD...

...SUPER CALM, THEN A TORRENT OF PASSION, FOLLOWED BY A LULL.

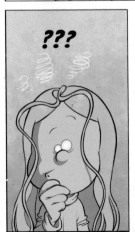

???

YOU'RE JUST A *BIG JERK*, MASON... YOU'VE BROKEN MY SISTER...

I CAN'T UNDERSTAND A WORD SHE SAYS NOW!

21

CAZENOVE & WILLIAM

WENDYYY... I FOUND LOTS OF *SCI-ANTI-FIG* EXPERIMENTS!

HAVE YOU NOTICED BEFORE THAT THE "S" IN THE WORD *"SNAIL"* IS MARKED ON ITS SHELL?

WOW!

WAIT, THAT'S NOT ALL!

WHEN YOU DUNK A ROLL OF PAPER TOWELS COMPLETELY INTO A TUB OF WATER, IT ABSORBS ALL THE LIQUID!

OH, MY GOSH!

AND WITH A BALLOON, DO YOU KNOW WHAT?

YOU PUT A *BAN-DAID* ON IT AND IT WON'T *BURST.*

≈PHEW...≈

AND BEST OF ALL IS THE *SOFT MUSIC* YOU CAN MAKE WITH A *PEN CAP!*

UH, WELL.

I'M GOING TO DO LOTS MORE OF THEM, THEN I WILL BE IN THE *ONE-CYCLOPEDIA* OF SCIENTISTS!

YEAH, YEAH... SURE, SURE...

!

LOOK AT *THIS*-- IT'S SO *STRONG...*

...A KEY IN THE SHAPE OF A HAMMER THAT OPENS EVERY LOCK!

Private Wendy Diary

22

CAZENOVE & WILLIAM

After heaps and heaps of mathematical calculations, I finally understand how **Wendy** works...

With my sister, her mood changes every other day...

The proof? Yesterday, she was dieting...

A salad and a glass of water, **Dad**, diet, you know...

And today, with her buds, she **stuffed** her face like an **Ogre!**

This barbecue sauce is sooo good!

SLURP

You want to finish my fries?

Yesterday her hair is totally **Awful**, today **it's the prettiest in the world**...

...which shows that she changes her mind **every** other day...

So, since I got rejected **yesterday**...

Wendy, will you give me your **private diary?** I haven't finished reading it.

Well, okay, it's not **always** every other day...!

MATH WHIZ

My Math Book

23

CAZENOVE & WILLIAM

PSSST

WENDY, HEY, WENDY...

...I'M A LITTLE COLD!

...MMPH...
...MMMOOUMPH...
I-IT'S OKAY...

THANKS-YOU'RE COOL!

SLEEPING IN MY BED, OKAY! STEALING MY COMFORTER-- NOT OKAYYYYY!

CAZENOVE & WILLIAM

WHENEVER THERE'S A STORM, *MAUREEN* BECOMES *UNBEARABLE*...

BROOOOOOOOOOOOOOOOOOOOOOOOO

OH, NOOOO...

SHE THROWS A HISSY FIT AND BAYS AT THE MOON...

THE LIGHTNING'S GOING TO FRY US ALL!

YOU KNOW, *MAUREEN*, I REALLY *LIKE* STORMS!

THAT'S 'CUZ THE LIGHTNING'S FRIED YOUR *BRAIN*!

LISTEN TO THE SOUND OF THE RAIN ON THE ROOF...

KAPOOM

ISN'T IT PLEASANT? AND THE GRAY SKY OUTSIDE...

I LOVE THIS AMBIENCE!

IF THE POWER GOES OUT, WE LIGHT LOTS OF CANDLES...

WHICH SMELL GOOD!

AND WE PLAY BOARD GAMES WAITING FOR IT TO BE OVER.

AH... YEAH!

SO, ISN'T ALL THAT GREAT?

TOTALLY!

BUT SHE'S *STILL* UNBEARABLE!

IT'S SO GREEEAAT!

WHEN'S THE NEXT STORM? WHEN IS IT?

WHEEEEN...?!

CAZENOVE & WILLIAM

WENDY, WENDY...WHY DOES EVERYONE HAVE A *SCARF* ON?

I HAVE NO TIME!

AND *YOU'VE* GOT A SCARF ON, TOO. SAY YOU'LL LEND IT TO ME?!

¿GRRR...¿ LEAVE ME ALONE, *LITTLE LEECH!*

COME ON, PRETTY PLEASE...

I WANT IT!

PRETTY PLEASE!

I WANT TO BE STYLISH, TOO!

IT'S SO CUTE! LEND IT TO ME!

COME ON, SHARE THE LOVE!

UMMM... YOUR SCARF'S COOL, *MAUREEN,* BUT IT'S WORN AROUND YOUR NECK, Y'KNOW!

OBVIOUSLY!

26

CAZENOVE & WILLIAM

I SWEAR TO YOU, *AUDREY*, I'VE FINALLY FOUND AN *ANTI-SISTER REPELLENT!*

AWWWESOME... TELL ME ABOUT IT, *WENDY!*

IT'S SOMETHING CRAZY. I TOSSED *THREE STINKY BALLS* AROUND MY BED.

HA-HA... THAT'S EXTREME!

WENDYYY...

EXACTLY. HERE'S THE LITTLE *TWIRP.* THIS IS GOING TO BE FUNNY...

BAM

⇒SNIFF⇐   ⇒SNIFF⇐

⇒SNIFF⇐   ⇒SNIFF⇐

YUCK! WHAT IS THAT *ROTTEN SMELL?*

I'M NOT STEPPING IN HERE ANYMORE.

LOL YEAHNN!

EW!

OH, BY THE WAY, I CAME TO TELL YOU YOUR *MASEY-WASEY'S* HERE.

NOOO ?!

WENDY... YOO-HOO, ARE YOU THERE?

PSHEEEE

PSHEEEE

PSHEEEEE

YES, UH, NO, UH, WAIT, *MASON...* I... ⇒GRRR...⇐

⇒SNIFF⇐ ARE YOU SICK? ⇒PFW⇐

27

CAZENOVE & WILLIAM

SO...
HAH!

...YOUR SISTER'S GREAT AT *TENNIS*...
YUP!

...NOT TO MENTION *BOWLING*...
...SHE KILLS IT!
HUNGH

LOOK AT THAT! IT'S AS IF SHE'D BEEN PLAYING *GOLF* ALL HER LIFE...
AWESOME!

...AND WHAT GREAT *BOXING* TECHNIQUE-- WOW!
≥HUF≤ ≥HUF≤ ≥HUF≤

AND *YOGA*, TOO!
SHE SERIOUSLY ROCKS IT!
PHOOOEEE

CLEARLY SHE'LL BE HARD TO BEAT...

...WHEN MY PARENTS DECIDE TO BUY US AN ACTUAL *WOOEE* GAME CONSOLE!

CAZENOVE & WILLIAM

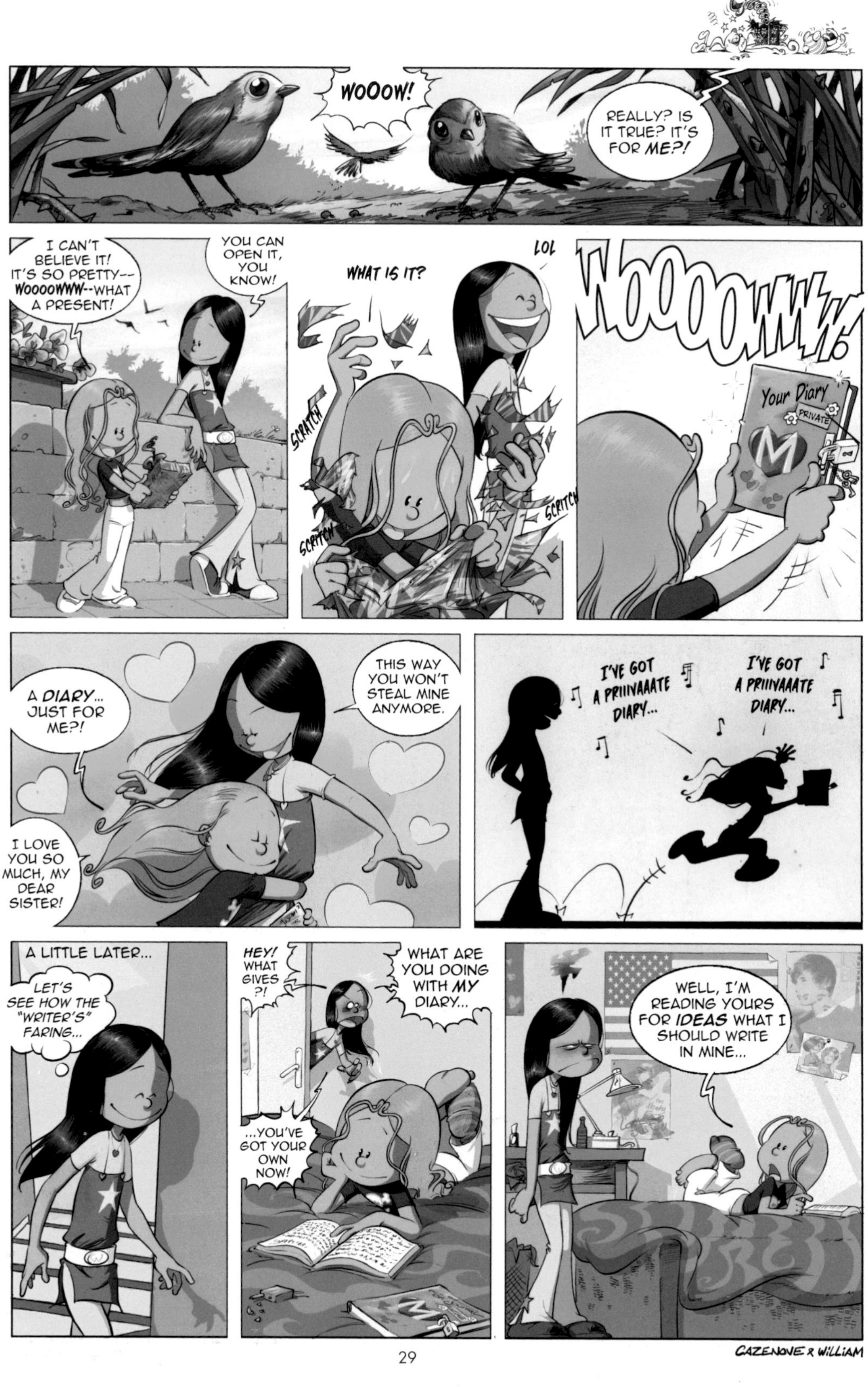

WOOOW!
REALLY? IS IT TRUE? IT'S FOR ME?!
I CAN'T BELIEVE IT! IT'S SO PRETTY-- WOOOOWWW--WHAT A PRESENT!
YOU CAN OPEN IT, YOU KNOW!
WHAT IS IT?
LOL
SCRATCH
SCRITCH
SCRITCH
WOOOOWWW!
Your Diary
PRIVATE
M
A DIARY... JUST FOR ME?!
THIS WAY YOU WON'T STEAL MINE ANYMORE.
I LOVE YOU SO MUCH, MY DEAR SISTER!
I'VE GOT A PRIIIVAAATE DIARY...
I'VE GOT A PRIIIVAAATE DIARY...
A LITTLE LATER...
LET'S SEE HOW THE "WRITER'S" FARING...
HEY! WHAT GIVES?!
WHAT ARE YOU DOING WITH MY DIARY...
...YOU'VE GOT YOUR OWN NOW!
WELL, I'M READING YOURS FOR IDEAS WHAT I SHOULD WRITE IN MINE...
CAZENOVE & WILLIAM

USUALLY, IT GOES LIKE *THIS*...

SNORE

MAUREEN, MAUREEN-- WAKE UP!

...WHEN OUR PARENTS TAKE US SOMEWHERE, WE LET MY SISTER KNOW AT THE LAST MINUTE...

...BECAUSE AS SOON AS SHE KNOWS, SHE BECOMES *INFURIATING*...

COME ON, GET UP. WE'RE GOING TO SPEND THE DAY AT THE AQUATIC PARK!

TO THE AT QUACK DUCK PARK?

FOR REAL?

YEP, THAT'S RIGHT.

YEEEAAAAHHHOOOOOOOOOO!

I LOVE THE *AT QUACK DUCK PARK!*

I TOTALLY AWESOME!

THEY'VE GOT WATER SLIDES!

I'LL GET TO GO ON ALL-NEW RIDES!

I NEED MY SUNSCREEN!

I NEED MY HANNAH MATTRESS SWIMSUIT!

MY SWIMSUIT! MY SWIMSUIT! MY SWIMSUIT!

THIS TIME, I LET HER KNOW 15 HOURS IN *ADVANCE*...

WENDYYYYY... COME HERE RIGHT NOW!

MY SWIMSUIT!

THAT'LL TEACH MOM AND *DAD* TO STOP ME FROM GOING TO THE MOVIES WITH MY BUDS!

HEH-HEH!

CAZENOVE & WILLIAM

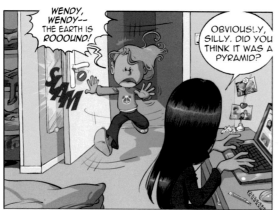
WENDY, WENDY-- THE EARTH IS ROOOUND!

OBVIOUSLY, SILLY. DID YOU THINK IT WAS A PYRAMID?

OH, YEAH? THEN WHY'S IT FLAT IN YOUR POSTER?

≳SIGH...≲ THAT HAS NOTHING TO DO WITH IT. THIS POSTER IS ONLY A ROLLED-OUT REPRESENTATION, YOU SEE...

...THAT WAY WE CAN SEE ALL THE COUNTRIES AT ONCE.

YOU'RE TRYING TO CONFUSE ME AGAIN?!

NOOOO.... LOOK...

...IF YOU ROLL IT UP LIKE THIS, IT BECOMES A GLOBE.

THERE YOU GO!

≳PFFFF...≲ THAT DOESN'T LOOK LIKE THE TEACHER'S GLOBE AT ALL...

WAIT...

...I JUST HAVE TO...

≳GRRRR...≲

...SLIDE TOGETHER ALREADY...

≳UGH!≲ I'M SICK OF THIS!

AREN'T YOU OVERREACTING?

HEY! OUCH!

ONCE AGAIN, YOU'VE GOTTEN ON MY NERVES!

HEEEYYY, YOU'RE ALMOST THERE-- LOOK!

SOME COUNTRIES JUST AREN'T IN THE SAME PLACES AS THEY ARE ON THE TEACHER'S GLOBE...

≳ARRRGH≲

NUMBSKULL!

CAZENOVE & WiLLiAM

Y'KNOW, LAST NIGHT I MADE A *PACT* WITH *MOM* AND *DAD*.

A *PACT*?! DO YOU EVEN KNOW WHAT THAT WORD MEANS?

UH-HUH! I PROMISED TO WORK SUPER HARD AT SCHOOL, AND YOU KNOW WHAT?

DON'T CARE.

COME ON, GUESS, GUESS, GUESS...

IN EXCHANGE, THEY OFFERED ME A *WOOEE* WITH A GAME AND JOYSTICKS!

HEH-HEH

HAH... YOU'VE SO BEEN *HAD!*

?

WHY DO YOU SAY THAT? THEY CAN'T LIE. THEY'RE *GROWNUPS!*

WELL, WHEN I WAS YOUR AGE I ALSO CAME TO AN AGREEMENT WITH OUR PARENTS...

AND?

THEY PROMISED ME THAT IF I WAS WELL-BEHAVED, I'D HAVE THE NICEST, CUTEST LITTLE SISTER...

WE BOTH KNOW HOW *THAT* TURNED OUT, SO I WOULDN'T TRUST THEIR PROMISES...!

HEE-HEE

≠HUMPH≠

CAZENOVE & WILLIAM

MAUREEN'S REALLY PATHETIC WITH HER *MR. BUN BUN*...

SO WHAT COLOR WAS HENRY IV'S *WHITE HORSE?*

YOU HAVEN'T DONE YOUR HOMEWORK!

SHE ACTS AS IF HE WERE *ALIVE*...

...AND A NICE PIECE OF TOAST WITH APRICOT AND BUTTER...

...WHICH YOU LOVE SO MUCH!

MOMMY, MR. BUN BUN FINISHED HIS SNACK AND HE REALLY LIKED IT!

IT'S MR. BUN BUN WHO MADE THIS MESS, *DADDY!*

I'M GOING TO PUNISH HIM!

IT'S JUST SO RIDICULOUS. ONE DAY I WILL TELL HER THAT MR. BUN BUN IS NOTHING MORE THAN A *STUFFED ANIMAL.*

KA-KRASH!

I *SWEAR* TO YOU, I DON'T KNOW WHAT GOT INTO MR. BUN BUN...HE HOPPED ONTO THE LAMP LIKE A *LUNATIC!*

≥MMFFF≤ ≥MMMM...≤

CAZENOVE & WILLIAM

DO YOU KNOW WHAT THIS IS, *MAUREEN?*

WELLLL, UH, IT LOOKS REALLY DISGUSTING!

IT'S A *COW'S EYE...*

...AND I'M GOING TO *EAT* IT.

YUCCKK! YOU'RE TOTALLY NUTSO, YOU KNOW!

CRACK
SLUUURP

YUMMM...

YIKES! MY SISTER'S TURNED INTO A *CANNONBALL...*

CALM DOWN. IT'S JUST AN EGG THAT I DREW A PUPIL ON. SEE?

DON'T TOUCH ME!

LOL! I REALLY HAD YOU GOING THERE, DIDN'T I?

OH, YEAAAHHH...IT REALLY IS AN EGG. GOOD JOKE, *WENDY!*

WASN'T IT?

I'M GOING TO PULL THIS TRICK ON *NAT* AND *MR. BUN BUN...*

...THEY'LL BE SCARED *STIFF!*

FIVE MINUTES LATER...

UMM... WENDY...

CAN YOU TELL ME AGAIN WHAT THE DIFFERENCE IS BETWEEN A HARD-BOILED EGG AND A *RAW* ONE?

CAZENOVE & WILLIAM

OOPS!

YIKES-- YOUR BRAND NEW *SOFA*...

...IF YOUR MOTHER'S LIKE MINE, YOU MIGHT AS WELL LEAVE THE COUNTRY, *WENDY*!

SPILL

DON'T WORRY. I'LL TAKE CARE OF IT!

I'VE WATCHED ENOUGH DETECTIVE SHOWS ON TV TO KNOW HOW TO ERASE *TRACE EVIDENCE*.

LOL

I CLEAN, SPONGE AND DRY... QUICK AS A FLASH!

WE SURE LEARN A LOT FROM TV.

KEROOOM

WENDYYYY... IT'S A *CATASTROPHE*... I BROKE *DADDYYY'S* BOTTLE OF INDIA INK...

AGAIN?! YOU REALLY LOOK FOR TROUBLE, DON'T YOU?

I TRIED TO CLEAN HIS DRAWINGS WITH SAND, TOO, BUT THAT MADE A TOTALLY DIRTY MESS!

AH-HA-HA!

NITWIT...

WHAT DO I DO, WENDY? WHAT DO I DO? WHAT DO I DO? WHAT DO I *DOOOOOOO*?

⸓SIGH...⸓

IT'S WORSE THAN A DISASTER FILM!

WAIT--I'VE GOT A BRILLIANT IDEA!

I'D BETTER SHAKE A LEG. DADDY'LL BE BACK SOON...

SO, YEAH, THAT'S WHAT HAPPENED. AN EARTHQUAKE HIT YOUR STUDIO...

...AND I DIDN'T EVEN HAVE TIME TO SAVE YOUR INDIA INK. CRAZY, ISN'T IT?

CLEARLY *MAUREEN* DOESN'T WATCH ENOUGH TV...

CAZENOVE & WILLIAM

KABLAM

AND THERE'S *FAIRYZILLA*, WHO DESTROYS THE CASTLE OF THAT ROTTEN *PRINCE CHARMING*...

MAUREEEEN!

DID YOU HAVE TO TELL *MOM* AND *DAD* THAT I GOT AN F IN MATH?!

I CAN'T BELIEVE IT...

SCREEECH

FAVORITE GIRL

...YOU'RE JUST A *TATTLE-TELLING* SNEAKER!

IT'S YOUR FAULT I HAVE TO CLEAN THE HOUSE FOR THE NEXT MONTH...

...AND I CAN'T USE MY COMPUTER, EITHER!

WHEN IT COMES TO BIG SNEAKS, YOU'RE SO BIG, YOU'RE *OFF-THE-SCALE* BIG!

NOT TRUE! NOT TRUE! NOT TRUUUE!

I'D RATHER LEAVE THE HOUSE THAN STAY INSIDE WITH THE *QUEEN OF BIG SNEAKS!*

FAV GIRL

I KNEW SHE WAS *WRONG!*

MY WEIGHT IS *NOT* OFF-THE-SCALE!

36

CAZENOVE & WILLIAM

EMMA'S MY SISTER **WENDY'S** NEW DANCE BUDDY...

ALL RIGHT, I'M READY.

WE'RE GOING TO HAVE A BLAST WITH THIS CHOREO-GRAPHY!

...BUT I DON'T *LIKE* EMMA.

BY THE WAY, I'VE BROUGHT YOU THE CD WE'LL BE DANCING TO...

COOL!

...AND YOU'LL SEE THERE'S SOME SONGS BY *JUSTIN BABY* THERE, TOO.

WOW--I'M SO INTO HIM. I CAN'T WAIT TO DANCE TO THEM!

I'M HIS BIGGEST FAN!

≈PFFFF...≈ WHAT A SHOW-OFF!

MY COUSIN MAY BE A BIGGER ONE. SHE TRAVELLED ALL OVER THE **STATES** TO SEE HIM ON TOUR.

REALLY? WISH I COULD DO THAT!

I WISH YOU WOULD LEAVE AND TRAVEL THE **SKATES**, TOO.

MY LITTLE SISTER'S GOING TO COME WATCH US DANCE. YOU'LL MEET HER.

≈MMM...?≈

SHE'S ADORABLE!

FINALLY SOMEONE WHO LIKES LITTLE SISTERS!

WELL, YOU'VE MET *MINE* ALREADY...

CAZENOVE & WILLIAM

YOU WON'T FORGET MY BIRTHDAY PARTY THIS SATURDAY, RIGHT WENDY?

NO WAY! I ALREADY KNOW WHAT I'M GOING TO WEAR...

A BIRTHDAY PARTAY?! I LOVE THOSE SO MUCH...

...BUT MS. BOSSY BOOTS NEVER LETS ME GO WITH HER!

UNLESS...

TA-DAH...

WHO'S THIRSTY?

CHERRY SODA...

...COOK-A-KOLA...

...AND EVEN ICE CUBES!

...FANTEE...

?!

I'D REALLY LIKE A KOLA, MAUREEN.

SAY, WOULD YOU LIKE TO COME TO MY BIRTHDAY PARTY, TOO?

I'M INVITED...? FOR REALS?!

OF COURSE!

HAVING FUN, WENDY?

HA-HA-HA, TOTALLY! I'VE NEVER HAD SUCH A GREAT TIME IN MY LIFE!

CAZENOVE & WILLIAM

38

WHAT'RE YOU DOING, WENDY?

CAN'T YOU TELL?

AUDREY AND EMMA ARE WAITING FOR ME SO WE CAN GO TO THE MOVIES BUT I'M NOT FINISHED.

THINK YOU'LL BE FASTER IF YOU VACUUM?

VUUUUM...

IT'S THESE LOUSY PANTS---THEY'RE REAL LINT COLLECTORS!

VUUUU UMMM...

IF MY BUDS SEE ME LIKE THIS, THEY'LL TEASE ME THE WHOLE NIGHT.

VUUUM...

THERE WE GO. ONCE OVER MY BUTT AND OFF I G--

VUUUMMM...

-NEEE-YA...-

HUH?! MAUREEN, WHAT ARE YOU DOING, NUTCASE?

SAY WHAT?

SPLISH

SPLISH

MOMMY ALWAYS SAYS TO MOP AFTER VACUUMING!

RATS! FOR ONCE, I REALLY WANTED TO CLEAN UP...

CAZENOVE & WILLIAM

THESE MOVIES ARE LOSERS!

YEAH, THEY'RE ALL CRAPPY!

ROMANCE FILMS GIVE ME THE HEEBIE-JEEBIES...

FILM NOIR, TOO.

I JUST WANT TO HAVE SOME LAUGHS. NOTHING GOOD'S PLAYING!

TOTALLY. IT WAS A TOUGH WEEK AT SCHOOL AND ALL I WANT IS TO CHILL OUT AND RELAX!

YOU SAID IT. BUT WE DON'T HAVE TO CHECK OUT A DUD TO HAVE FUN, GIRLS...

...WE COULD GO TO MY PLACE!

WE'LL HAVE A BLAST, GUARANTEED!

DO YOU HAVE ANY NEW DVDs?

WELL, ISN'T THIS FUNNY?

HA-HA-HA

YES... HEE-HEE-HEE

IT AIN'T ME...

IT AIN'T ME... IT AIN'T ME...

CAZENOVE & WILLIAM

BEEP BEEP BEEP BEEP BEEP

≥YAAAWWWN...≤

BEEP BEEP BEEP BEEP BEEP

≥GRUMPH!≤ WHAT IS THAT *NOISE?!*

IS THAT YOUR ALARM, *MAUREEN?*

WELL, I'VE GOT SCHOOL TODAY.

SO DO I, BUT IT'S *FOUR O'CLOCK IN THE MORNING!*

BEEP CLICK

I'VE GOT LOTS OF ODDS-AND-ENDS TO TAKE CARE OF...

SCRATCH-SCRATCH

YOU MEAN *IN ADDITION* TO KEEPING ME FROM *SLEEPING?!*

BEFORE TAKING MY BATH, I HAVE TO GET *MR. BUN BUN* READY...

...BRUSH HIM, COMB HIM AND PUT COLOGNE ON HIM.

THAT ONLY TAKES YOU *FIVE MINUTES*--

--YOU DON'T NEED TO GET UP SO CRAZY EARLY!

NO, BUT DO YOU THINK I'VE ONLY GOT MR. BUN BUN TO TAKE CARE OF?!

41

CAZENOVE & WILLIAM

 YIIIKES...! TELL ME YOU *DIDN'T* JUST DO THAT!

 YUP, I ALSO BROKE ANOTHER BOTTLE OF *DADDY'S* INDIA INK BUT BE *QUIET!* HE'S GOING TO HEEEAAAR...

SHHHHH...

OKAY, BUT I TOLD YOU *NOT* TO CRAWL AROUND IN HIS OFFICE!

PSHEEE...

 DON'T TELL HIM, OKAY?

WE'LL *SEE...*

WENDY?! YOU WON'T SAY ANYTHING, *RIGHT?*

 SURE, BUT ONLY ON *ONE* CONDITION...

 ...YOU'LL SET THE TABLE FOR ME FOR A MONTH...

...THEN I'LL HAVE YOUR COMPUTER TIME FOR A WHOLE WEEK...

MMMM... FINE!

...YOU'LL MAKE MY BED, TOO...

PSHEEEE...

 ...YOU WON'T GO INTO MY ROOM ANYMORE, ESPECIALLY WHEN MY FRIENDS ARE HERE...

GRUMPH!

PSHEEEE...

YEAH YEAH YEAH

...YOU WON'T TOUCH MY MAKEUP CASE...

 ...AND, FINALLY, YOU'LL GIVE ME YOUR CHOCOLATE MO--

--AAAH!

 WHAT'RE YOU DOING, NOW?!

WELL, SINCE I AGREE TO ALL YOUR DEMANDS, I'M GOING TO MISBEHAVE TO THE *MAX!*

CAZE JOVE & WILLIAM

BEFORE TACKLING *SCUBA DIVING*, YOU'LL FIRST HAVE TO GET USED TO SWIMMING WEARING ALL THIS EQUIPMENT...

WENDY, WE'LL SINK LIKE ROCKS IF WE DIVE WITH ALL THESE *DUMB THINGS* ON US!

NO, *MAUREEN*, IT'S TO *AVOID* DROWNING.

BUT WE CAN'T EVEN WALK WITH THESE *PENGUIN FEET*...

COME ON, GIRLS, LET'S GET TO THE END OF THE DOCK.

YOU JUST HAVE TO RUIN MY DAY AGAIN, DON'T YOU!

NYAH-NYAH-NYAH-NYAH

HUH?

SLURPPP

SPLOOSH

GLUB-GLUB

?!

HEEELLLPPPP... I'M SINKING...I'M DROWWWWNING TOO!

UMM, WENDY. ALTERNATIVELY, WE OFFER AN *INTRODUCTION TO PING-PONG* NEXT DOOR.

≶SIGH...≶

TITANIC

CAZENOVE & WILLIAM

‹ HMMPH... ›
I'M GOING
TO WIN!

LOL! GO BUY
YOURSELF SOME
REAL LEGS FIRST,
HEDGEHOPPER!

GOING
BACKWARDS
WORKS,
TOO.

NO FAIR!
YOU WERE
ELIMINATED!

I WON
FIRSTIES!
THE SWING'S
MIIINE!

YOU'RE
ROTTEN!

BESIDES, IT WAS
MY IDEA TO RACE
FOR THE SWING!

THEN YOU
SHOULD HAVE
GOTTEN HERE
BEFORE ME!

♪ LA-LA-
LA-LA ♪

THIS'S
CRUDDY!

I WANT
TO SWING
SO BAD...

I WANT
TO SWING!

I WANT
TO SWING!

I WANT
TO SWING!

I WANT TO SWIIII

FWOOSH

MAUREEN!

‹ SIGH ›
WHEN
YOU GET
SOMETHING
IN YOUR
HEAD...

‹ TSK
TSK... ›

CAZENOVE & WILLIAM

TEE-HEE...

HIYA...
DID YOU FORGET WHAT TIME IT IS?

DID YOU PARTY ALL NIGHT, OR WHAT?!

COME ON, DRINK YOUR COFFEE.

HURRY, OR WE'RE GOING TO BE LATE FOR SCHOOL!

?

COME ONNNN ALREADY! UPSY-DAISY...

WE'RE GOING TO MISS THE BUS!

:SNICKER...:

?!

PFRRR...

MWAH-HA-HA

HA-HA-HA

WE REALLY GOT YOU!

IT'S SUNDAY! GET IT? HEE-HEE-HEE!

SCHOOL BUS STOP

THEY'VE GOT NO SENSE OF HUMOR!

TOTALLY!

VROOOOOM...

CAZENOVE & WILLIAM

UMM... YOU'RE SURE YOUR SISTER ISN'T AROUND?

IF SHE SEES US, WE'RE DEAD!

IF WENDY ISN'T IN FRONT OF THE TV, IN FRONT OF THE MIRROR, OR IN FRONT OF THE FRIDGE, IT'S BECAUSE SHE ISN'T HERE!

AND NOW, WELCOME TO WENDYLAND!

SO CLASSY!

I LOVE HER BED!

LOOK AT THE THREADS SHE'S GOT!

LOOK, MAUREEN, I'M A REAL ADOLESCENT.

LOL! YOU'RE JUST MISSING PIMPLES ON YOUR FACE!

HER MUSIC'S GREAT!

YUP. IT'S AARON BEE!

YO-YO- OYO!

AND LOOK AT ALL THE DVDS SHE'S--

MAUREEN, WHERE ARE YOU GOING? YOU DON'T WANT TO GO THROUGH YOUR SISTER'S THINGS ANYMORE?

YES, LULU, BUT I'M CALLING HER SO THAT SHE'LL COME BACK...

...IT'S MUCH LESS FUN WHEN YOU KNOW YOU CAN'T GET CAUGHT!

46

CAZENOVE & WILLIAM

WHAT ARE ALL THESE *FIBS?!*

DID YOU MESS UP MY DIARY OR WHAT?!

YOU WERE SUPPOSED TO LEARN THAT POEM TODAY. IT'S REALLY NO BIG DEAL...

AND YOU DON'T KNOW IT EITHER, *PANDY?*

WELL, THAT'S JUST GREAT!

DO YOU HAVE A NOTE FROM YOUR PARENTS?

NOT EVEN THAT?

PFFF... YES, I'VE GOT A BUNCH OF *IGNORE AMUSES.*

YOU DIDN'T HAVE ENOUGH TIME? YEAH, SURE...I DON'T BELIEVE YOU.

DON'T PUSH IT...

IT'S BEEN A WEEK SINCE I TOLD YOU THERE'D BE A SURPRISE QUIZ!

NOW YOU MAY STAND IN THE CORNER...

THAT'LL TEACH YOU TO IGNORE YOUR ASSIGNMENTS!

MAUREEN, YOU GOT A ZERO!

NOW YOU MAY STAND IN THE CORNER... THAT'LL TEACH YOU TO IGNORE YOUR ASSIGNMENTS!

COPYCAT!

47

CAZENOVE & WILLIAM

HEY, YOU KNOW THE ELEVATOR'S NOT JUST FOR WIMPS?!

YEAH, BUT I CAN'T QUITE REMEMBER WHAT FLOOR IT'S ON ANYMORE!

BESIDES, YOU AREN'T GOING TO BUTT IN... IT'S *YOUR* FAULT I HAD TO SET UP THIS DOCTOR'S APPOINTMENT!

BARRY WEINSTEIN, PHD. BARAKA

SPECIALIST

≈HISSS...≈

MISS MAUREEN...

IT'S OUR TURN. HURRY UP!

OUR?

SO YOU HAVE A LITTLE SPOT ON YOUR LEG, CORRECT?

LITTLE? IT'S *ENORMOUS!*

WHAT A *WUSS!*

MMM-HMMM... ACTUALLY...

...I'VE NEVER SEEN ANYTHING LIKE IT! HOW DID THIS HAPPEN?

YOU SHOULD ASK MY SISTER ABOUT THAT...

ARE YOU *NUTS* OR WHAT, *MAUREEN?* AREN'T YOU SICK OF BLAMING ME?!

NOPE... I REMEMBER IT ALL TOO WELL, *WENDY...*

THAT WOULD SURPRISE ME AS YOUR MEMORY RUNS LIKE A *SIEVE!*

UMMM...

YOU'RE JUST A *DIRTY LIAR,* FOR STARTERS!

NO, YOU ARE!

OH, I KNOW WHAT I'LL WRITE ON IT...

HEYYY, DON'T PRESS SO HARD. IT HURTS...

...YOU'RE GOING TO GO THROUGH THE CAST!

REALLY? JEEZ, YOU CAN BE SUCH A *WUSS!*

48

CAZENOVE & WILLIAM

WHEN I WANT TO TELL SOMEONE A SECRET, I'VE GOT **LOTS** OF CHOICES...

...OF COURSE, THERE'S MY SISTER **WENDY** AND I KNOW SHE WON'T TELL EVEN HER BEST BUDS...

IT'S THE SAME WITH **MOMMY.** WHEN I TELL HER A SECRET, IT'S SAFER THAN THE HUGEST SAFE FILLED WITH CASH ON EARTH!

...**DADDY** WOULDN'T SAY ANYTHING EITHER...

BESIDES, I'M NOT EVEN SURE HE EVEN REMEMBERS THEM.

CREAK

ZZZZ

THEN THERE'S **MR. BUN BUN...** I TOTALLY TRUST HIM.

BUT IN GENERAL, I TELL MY BIGGEST SECRETS TO **NAT.**

WHISPER WHISPER WHISPER

NOOO?!

YES!

HONESTLY, WHAT'S THE POINT OF HAVING A SECRET IF NO ONE KNOWS ABOUT IT?!

WHISPER WHISPER WHISPER

CAZENOVE & WILLIAM

BLAH BLAH BLAH BLAH BLAH

AND SO ON AND SO FORTH

DID THEY REALLY STOP TALKING BECAUSE OF ME?

HMM... I'LL TRY AGAIN...

YOU'RE REALLY *ROTTEN!*

AND *MEAN!*

AND IT'S ALL 'CUZ YOU'RE PLOTTING AGAINST ME, RIGHT?!

I HAAAATE ALL OF YOU!

DO YOU *STILL* WANT US TO COME UP WITH AN IDEA FOR A BIRTHDAY PRESENT FOR *MAUREEN?*

NO WAY!

CAZENOVE & WILLIAM

HAVING **WENDY** IN A CLOTHING STORE IS TOTALLY **AWFUL**...

YEAH!

GO CLASSY!

...SHE TAKES THREE YEARS TO MAKE UP HER MIND...

UH, **SAMMIE**--IN YOUR OPINION?

TRY ON **ALL** OF THEM. THAT'LL BE EASIEST!

AND HA-HA-HAH-HA-HA, THE SCARF IS TOO LONG...

MEH!

DON'T WORRY, WE'LL FIGURE IT OUT!

...AND THE JACKET, HA-HA-HAH-HA-HA, IT'S TOO BLUE...≶PFFF≶...

YUCK. THE COLOR KILLS THE STYLE!

AND THE **SHOES**, HA-HA-HAH-HA-HA, THE LACES ARE TOO BIG...

WENDY, DO YOU WANT TO CATCH A MOVIE TONIGHT?

A MOVIE?! I'LL GO!

I'LL GO! I'LL GO! I'LL GO! I'LL GO! HEY, WENDY, MAY I GO?!

NO!

YEAH, WELL, SOMETIMES SHE MAKES UP HER MIND **TOO QUICKLY**!

51

CAZENOVE & WILLIAM

AH, YOU'RE HERE, *WENDY*...

...I WAS LOOKING *EVERYWHERE* FOR YOU!

I'M GOING TO GIVE YOU A PRESENT. BUT FIRST, YOU HAVE TO PROMISE TO KEEP IT.

≈MMMNNN≈... ≈GRUMPH≈...

YOU'RE NOT ALLOWED TO THROW IT *OUT*, PUT IT *DOWN*, GIVE IT *AWAY*, OR PUT IT IN YOUR PURSE, OKAY?

OTHERWISE, IT'S NOT WORTH IT.

≈SIGH≈

TA-DAAAH!

AND HEEEERE IT IS...A PRESENT FOR YOU!

HONESTLY! YOU THINK THAT--

YOU *PROMISED*. YOU HAVE TO HOLD IT IN YOUR HAND, ALWAYS!

ARE WE GOOD?!

YES, HEE-HEE-HEE...

SHE DOESN'T SUSPECT A THING. WE'LL HEAR *EVERYTHING* MY SISTER AND HER BOYFRIEND SAY!

I BROUGHT SOMETHING TO TAKE NOTES WITH!

ARE YOU *AN ONLY CHILD*, I HOPE?!

CAZENOVE & WILLIAM

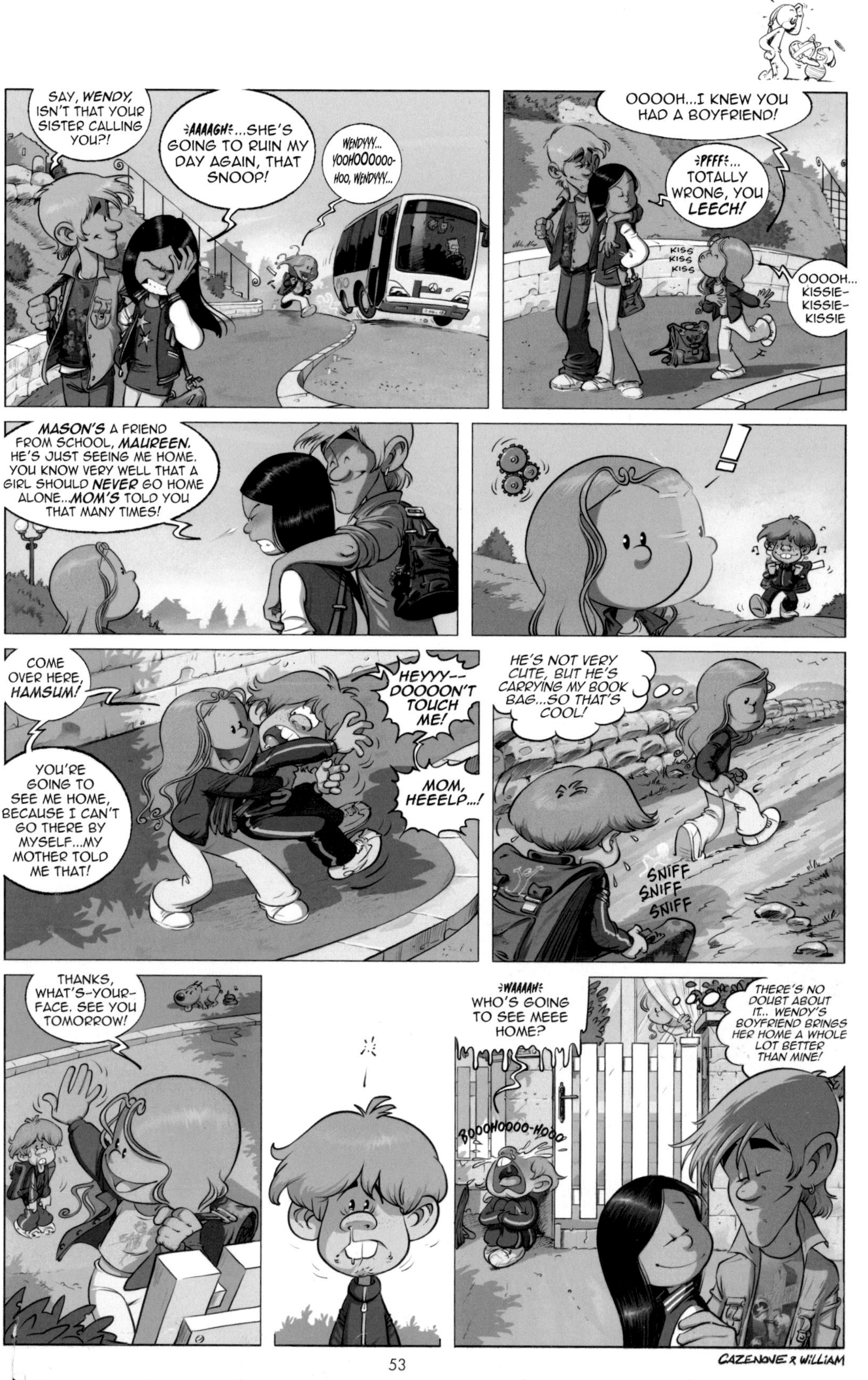
SAY, WENDY, ISN'T THAT YOUR SISTER CALLING YOU?!
AAAAGH...SHE'S GOING TO RUIN MY DAY AGAIN, THAT SNOOP!
WENDYYY... YOOHOOOOOO-HOO, WENDYYY...
OOOOH...I KNEW YOU HAD A BOYFRIEND!
PFFF... TOTALLY WRONG, YOU LEECH!
KISS KISS KISS
OOOOH... KISSIE-KISSIE-KISSIE
MASON'S A FRIEND FROM SCHOOL, MAUREEN. HE'S JUST SEEING ME HOME. YOU KNOW VERY WELL THAT A GIRL SHOULD NEVER GO HOME ALONE...MOM'S TOLD YOU THAT MANY TIMES!
!
COME OVER HERE, HAMSUM!
YOU'RE GOING TO SEE ME HOME, BECAUSE I CAN'T GO THERE BY MYSELF...MY MOTHER TOLD ME THAT!
HEYYY--DOOOON'T TOUCH ME!
MOM, HEEELP...!
HE'S NOT VERY CUTE, BUT HE'S CARRYING MY BOOK BAG...SO THAT'S COOL!
SNIFF SNIFF SNIFF
THANKS, WHAT'S-YOUR-FACE. SEE YOU TOMORROW!
WAAAAH WHO'S GOING TO SEE MEEE HOME?
BOOOHOOOO-HOOO
THERE'S NO DOUBT ABOUT IT... WENDY'S BOYFRIEND BRINGS HER HOME A WHOLE LOT BETTER THAN MINE!
CAZENOVE & WILLIAM

WENDY HAS A SUPER-STRANGE OBSESSION-- SHE ONLY EATS *TOMATOES*...

...NOTHING AT DINNER EXCEPT THE ONES SHE JUGGLES AND SWALLOWS...

CHOMP
YUM
CHOMP

AND FOR DESSERT, WHAT DOES SHE EAT? A BOWL OF CHERRY TOMATOES... EVEN WHEN WE'VE GOT CHOCOLATE CAKE...

SHE DOESN'T EVEN GIVE THEM TIME TO RIPEN IN THE GARDEN...

AAAH! LOVELY!

MAUREEN, GO GET YOUR SISTER TO CLEAR THE TABLE, PLEASE.

YES, *MOM!*

WEEENDYYY...

YOU NEED TO CLE--

MOMMY, I THINK SHE WON'T BE ABLE TO COME... SHE'S KISSIE-KISSING HER BOYFRIEND!

YOU SHOULD STOP WITH THE TOMATOES, Y'KNOW... YOU'RE STARTING TO LOOK LIKE THEM!

BWAH-HA

CAZENOVE & WILLIAM

MAUREEEEEEN... GET A MOVE ON-- WE'RE GOING TO MISS THE START OF THE CONCERT BECAUSE OF YOU!

I'M SOOO EXCITED TO GO SEE *ISAYA LEEK* ALIVE...

...I SAVED MY ALLOWANCE TO BUY LOTSA SOUVENIRS!

UM, IT'S A CONCERT, NOT AN ARTISANAL FAIR.

YOU'RE TALKING NONSENSE!

BESIDES, WE'RE DRAGGING YOU ALONG WITH US. CONSIDER THIS A PRESENT.

ARE YOU GOING TO START BEING A PAIN?!

TALK ABOUT A PRESENT—ME PUTTING UP WITH *YOU* THE WHOLE EVENING!

YOU'RE THE ONE WHO'S JUST A EEEGOIST!

OH, YEAH?!

WELL, YOU'RE JUST A *DIMWIT!*

YOU'RE THE ONE WHO'S A *DIMMED TWIT!*

THAT'S IT! WE'RE NOT GOING TO THE CONCERT!

GO TO YOUR ROOMS!

THIS IS YOUR FAULT, *DUMMY!*

YOUR BRAIN'S *ROTTED OUT!*

I'M GOING TO PULL OUT YOUR BABY TEETH!

YOU'RE NOT MY SISTER ANYMORE!

AS A RESULT, THERE WERE *TWO* CONCERTS IN TOWN THAT EVENING...

55

CAZENOVE & WILLIAM

YOU'RE LUCKY YOU FOUND A BOYFRIEND...

...I'D REALLY LIKE TO HAVE ONE, TOO, Y'KNOW...

...BUT I THINK I'M TOO HARD TO PLEASE!

MY IDEAL BOYFRIEND SHOULD BE...

...EXTRA LOVING...

...AND CUDDLY AS ALL GET OUT... BUT REALLY FUNNY, TOO...

...AND HE SHOULD TELL ME HE LOVES ME EVERY DAY... AND NOT JUST ONCE...

LOL!

YEAH, WELL, I KNOW I'M ASKING FOR TOO MUCH...

OH, NO--NOT AT ALL!

I'LL LEND HIM TO YOU UNTIL YOU HAVE TIME TO GET YOURSELF ONE...THERE'RE TONS MORE IN THE TOY STORES!

GIVE ME A HUG!

I LOVE YOU!

HA HA

HA

56

CAZENOVE & WILLIAM

WENDY, CAN I ASK YOU SOMETHING?

NO THANKS.

DO YOU THINK I SHOULD GET RID OF MR. BUN BUN?

WELL, YOU MAY BE A LITTLE TOO OLD FOR HIM, NOW

YOU KNOW...

...THE BIGGER YOU GET, THE LESS YOU'LL FEEL THE NEED TO BE STUCK TO THAT STINKY RABBIT!

OH, BUT HOW WILL I KNOW WHEN IT'S THE RIGHT TIME?

SET YOURSELF A GOAL...A CUT-OFF DATE.

HEYYY, I DON'T WANT TO BUMP HIM OFF. ARE YOU SOFT IN THE HEAD OR WHAT?

LOL! NO...

JUST TELL YOURSELF, "AFTER SUCH-AND-SUCH A DATE, I'LL STOP TAKING MR. BUN BUN WITH ME." THERE YOU HAVE IT!

THAT'LL HELP YOU MAKE A DECISION.

OH, YES?

MAKE A DECISION...

MAKE A DECISION...

ACTUALLY, I KNOW WHAT I'M GOING TO DO, WENDY...

WELL, IT'S ABOUT TIME!

I'LL GET RID OF MR. BUN BUN WHEN YOU GET RID OF YOURS!

IT'LL BE EASIER IF WE QUIT TOGETHER!

CAZENOVE & WILLIAM

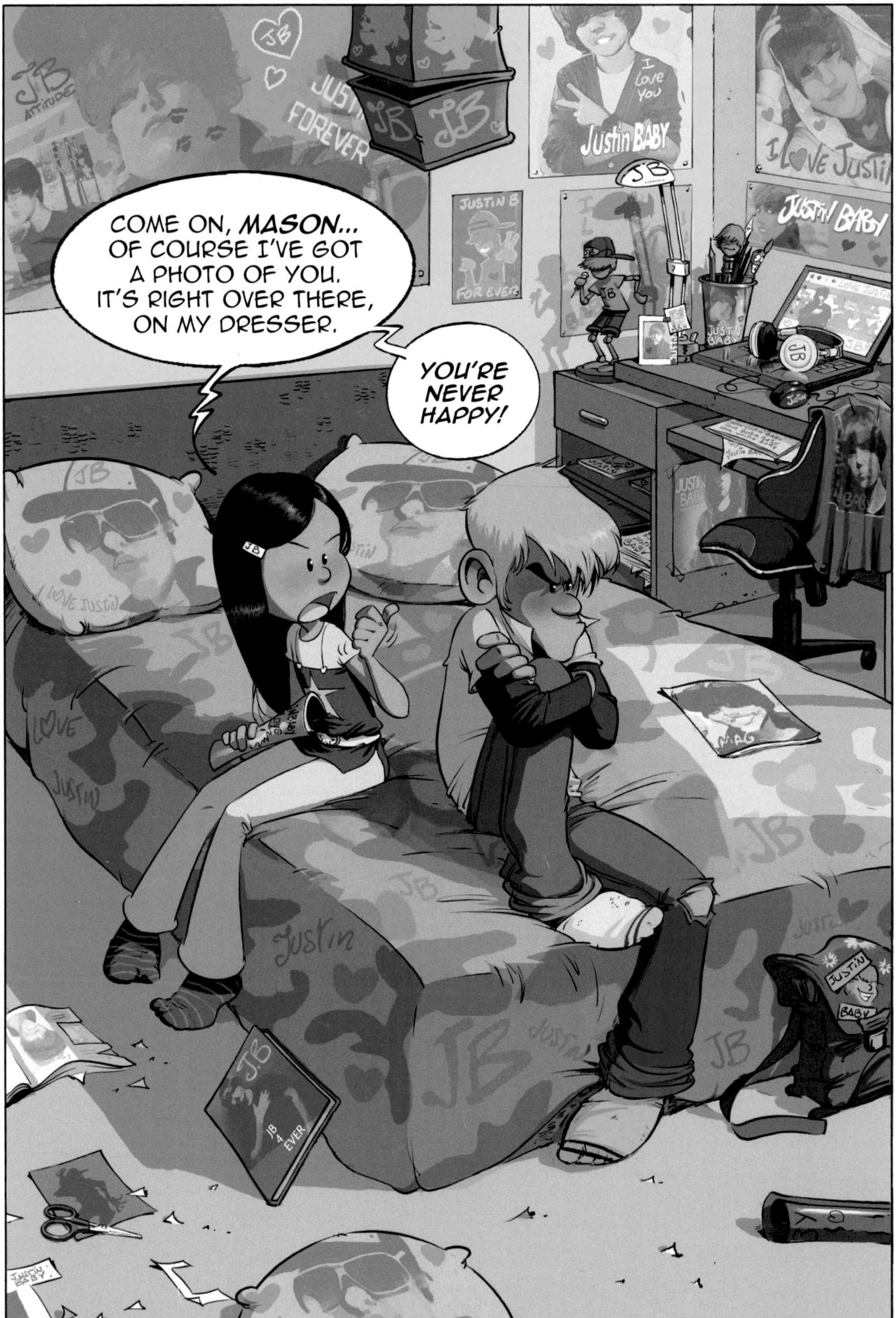
COME ON, MASON... OF COURSE I'VE GOT A PHOTO OF YOU. IT'S RIGHT OVER THERE, ON MY DRESSER.
YOU'RE NEVER HAPPY!
JUSTIN FOREVER
I love you
Justin BABY
I LOVE JUSTIN
JUSTIN BABY
JUSTIN B
FOR EVER
JB 4 EVER
MAG

CAZENOVE & WILLIAM

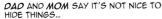
DAD AND **MOM** SAY IT'S NOT NICE TO HIDE THINGS...

THEY SAY THAT A FAULT CONFESSED IS HALF REDRESSED...

COME ON, **MAUREEN**--GO FOR IT!

HEY, THERE... HEE-HEE...SAY, **WENDY**... UH, WEREN'T YOU LOOKING FOR ME?

NO, WHY?

WELL, 'CUZ I USED SCISSORS TO CUT UP YOUR FAVORITE PICTURE WITH **MASON**--EVEN THOUGH I DIDN'T DO IT ON-PURPOSE... **WELL**, NOT REALLY... WELL, MAYBE A LITTLE BIT.

ARE YOU **MAD** AT ME?

≈SIGH≈ I'M TOO OLD FOR THIS CHILDISHNESS, YOU KNOW...

...PLUS, I PICKED MY PRETTIEST TOP TO WEAR TO GO SHOPPING WITH **AUDREY**. SO DO YOU THINK I'M GOING TO SPOIL ALL THAT JUST TO JUMP ON YOU AND GIVE YOU A THRASHING?

THAT'S TRUE. YOU FORGIVE ME?

NO!

IN YOUR DREAMS!

≈GASP!≈

IN SHORT...DAD AND MOM JUST TALK **NONSENSE!**

CAZENOVE & WILLIAM

WENDY, MY FAVORITE SISTER, I'M BORROWING YOUR ERASER WITH THE SPARKLES IN IT.

OKAY, BUT DON'T FORGET IT'S GOT MY NAME ON IT!

WOOOOUUUUW!!

MOMMY, YOUR PEN LIGHT'S SO COOL. WILL YOU LEND IT TO ME?

OKAY, BUT IT'S GOT MY NAME ON IT!

HEY, THERE!

THAT TRANSPARENT TAPE'S GOT MY NAME ON IT!

...IT'S GOT MY NAME ON IT...

...IT'S GOT MY NAME ON IT...

...IT'S GOT MY NAME ON IT...

BEEP BEEP BEEP

RATS! HOW COME WHEN I BUY STUFF, MY NAME ISN'T ON IT?

SALE

DO NOT TOUCH

CAZENOVE & WILLIAM

THIS IS A SUPER POWERFUL TACTIC I SAW IN A MOVIE. IT WORKS EVERY TIME...

BABY BABY

LULU GETS **WENDY** TO BELIEVE I'M MEMORIZING HER PRIVATE DIARY...

THAT PEST!

‡GRRRR‡...

WENDY GOES UP TO HER ROOM AT FULL SPEED BUT IT'S **EMPTY**...

‡GRRRUMBLL‡...

WENDY CONFIRMS THAT HER BELOVED PRIVATE DIARY IS STILL IN ITS SUPER PRIVATE HIDING PLACE...

‡PHEW!‡

WENDY LEAVES, COMPLETELY REASSURED...

THEN I COME OUT FROM MY SUPER HIDEOUT UNDER THE BED, AND NOW I KNOW WHERE HER BELOVED DIARY IS!

NYUCK-NYUCK-NYUCK!

IT'S WORTH WATCHING TV SOMETIMES...

...TOO BAD I FORGOT I SAW THAT MOVIE WITH WENDY...

CAZENOVE & WILLIAM

MAUREEN'S PICKED UP A NEW HABIT...

"CHUCKLING COW" OR "NULTELA" FOR MY SNACK.

EENIE, MEENIE, MINY, MOE...THUMP A TIGER ON THE TOE... WHEN HE THUMPS BACK DON'T BE SLOW... EENIE, MEENIE, MINY, MOE!

CHOMP

IT'S THE SAME THING WHEN SHE'S CHOOSING A DVD.

EENIE, MEENIE, MINY, MOE...THUMP A TIGER ON THE TOE... IF HE THUMPS BACK...

...A COMICBOOK, TOO...

EENIE, MEENIE, MINY, MOE, THUMP A TIGER ON THE TOE, EENIE, MEENIE, MINY, MOE...

THRUM THRUM

HERE, MAUREEN, TRY IT WITH THIS.

WITH A QUARTER?

THERE'S NOTHING BETTER THAN HEADS OR TAILS FOR CHOOSING BETWEEN TWO OPTIONS, YOU KNOW.

OH, WELL. IT LANDED PERFECTLY. I WOULD'VE HAD TROUBLE CHOOSING BETWEEN LISTENING TO THIS CD BY *KATY PUREE* OR THIS OTHER ONE BY *ISAYA*.

SUPER COOL!

UH... ON THE OTHER HAND, SHOULD I LET IT ROLL OR TOSS IT INTO THE AIR?

HMM...

EENIE, MEENIE, MINY, MOE... THUMP A TIGER ON HIS TOE... EENIE, MEENIE, MINY MOE...

CAZENOVE & WILLIAM

WHAT'S THAT RACKET, *MAUREEN?*

DON'T KNOW, BUT IT'S A TOTAL *PAIN!*

NOOOO... A HERD OF *BOYS*...

...AND IN MY HOUSE, TOO!

WHY'S *WENDY* INVITING BOYS TO THE HOUSE? DOES SHE HAVE A SCREW LOOSE, OR WHAT?

PLUS BOYS AREN'T GOOD FOR ANYTHING...

...THEY'RE ALWAYS PLAYING FOOTBALL...

...OR NINTENDOX IN FRONT OF THE TV.

THEY DON'T SMELL GOOD...

...THEY'RE A BUNCH OF CROCKS LIKE SOCKS...

...THEY'RE NOISY...

...AND WORSE, THEY'RE *STRONGER* THAN GIRLS!

A-HA! THAT'S IT, *LULU!* WENDY'S GOING TO MOVE OUT AND SHE NEEDS LOTS OF GUYS TO HELP CARRY THE BOXES!

HEY, I'D REALLY LIKE TO HELP YOU WITH YOUR MOVE, BUT WHEN'RE YOUR FRIENDS GOING TO LEND *US* A HAND?

CAZENOVE & WILLIAM

SO, DO YOU KNOW IF *EMMA'S* COMING WITH US TO THE MOVIES?

NO, I NEED TO ASK HER.

I THOUGHT YOU'D SENT HER A TEXT.

NOT WORTH IT.

WHY? DOESN'T SHE HAVE HER CELL PHONE ANYMORE? DID HER PARENTS TAKE IT?

WHAT A TRAGEDY!

NO, IT'S NOT THAT.

IF NOT, WE COULD GO TO HER PLACE...

...SHE DOESN'T LIVE FAR FROM HERE.

DON'T WORRY ABOUT IT, *SAMMIE.* I'VE ACTUALLY GOT SOMETHING A LOT FASTER THAN THAT.

FASTER THAN AN SMS? WELL, LET'S SEE. YOU MUST THINK I'M AN *IDIOT.*

NO, OF COURSE NOT. IT'S CALLED AN "MSM"!

A WHAT?

SO... ⸝PANT⸝ ⸝PHEW⸝...I ALSO KNOW THAT WENDY AND SAMMIE WOULD LIKE TO KNOW IF YOU WANT TO GO...

...WITH THEM TO THE MOVIES... ⸝PHEW⸝...

AND SO ON AND SO FORTH...

AN "MSM": *MY SISTER MAUREEN!*

64

CAZENOVE & WILLIAM

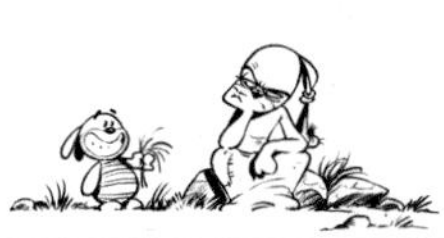

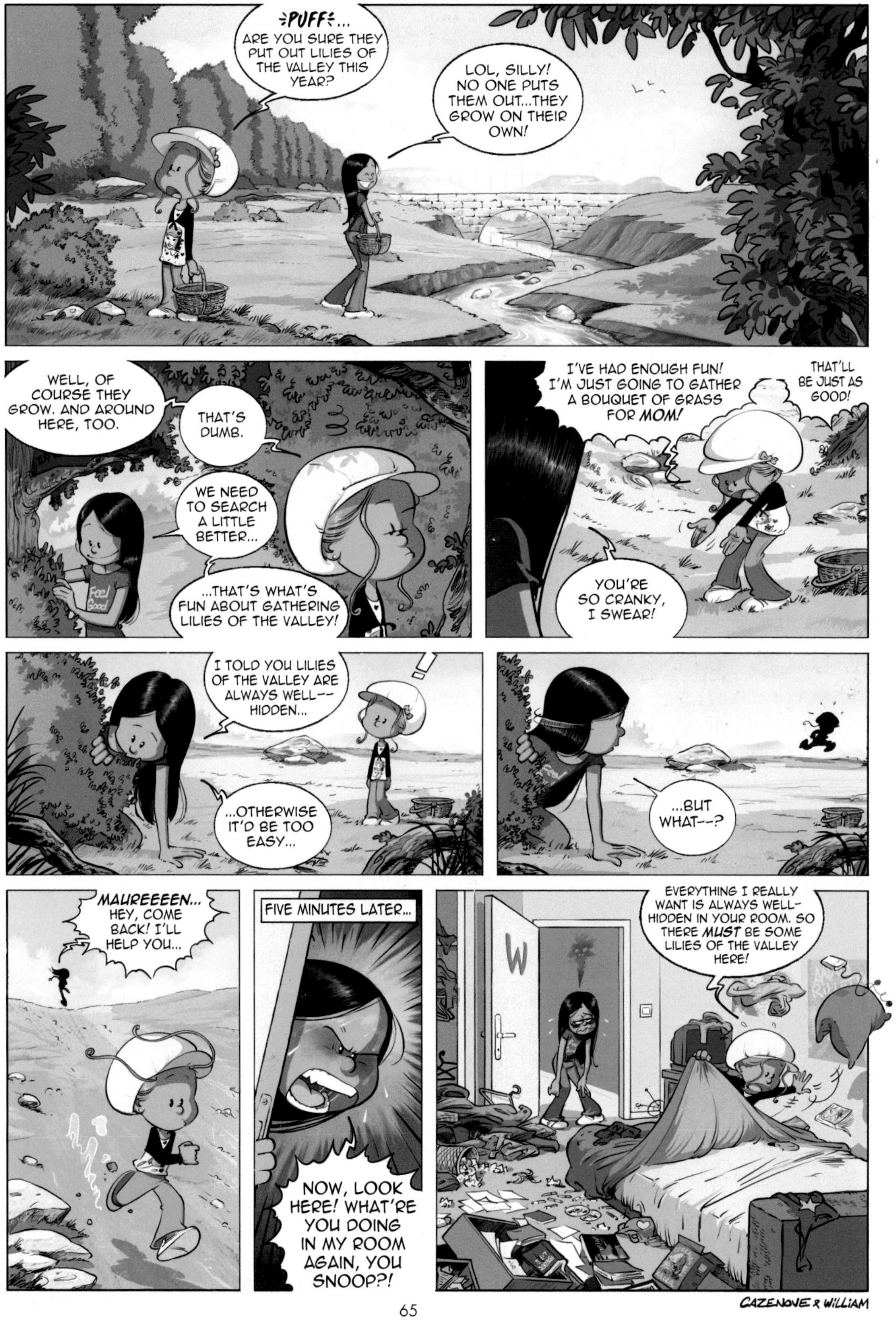
PUFF...
ARE YOU SURE THEY PUT OUT LILIES OF THE VALLEY THIS YEAR?
LOL, SILLY! NO ONE PUTS THEM OUT...THEY GROW ON THEIR OWN!
WELL, OF COURSE THEY GROW. AND AROUND HERE, TOO.
THAT'S DUMB.
WE NEED TO SEARCH A LITTLE BETTER...
...THAT'S WHAT'S FUN ABOUT GATHERING LILIES OF THE VALLEY!
Feel Good
I'VE HAD ENOUGH FUN! I'M JUST GOING TO GATHER A BOUQUET OF GRASS FOR MOM!
THAT'LL BE JUST AS GOOD!
YOU'RE SO CRANKY, I SWEAR!
I TOLD YOU LILIES OF THE VALLEY ARE ALWAYS WELL-- HIDDEN...
...OTHERWISE IT'D BE TOO EASY...
!
...BUT WHAT--?
MAUREEEEN... HEY, COME BACK! I'LL HELP YOU...
FIVE MINUTES LATER...
NOW, LOOK HERE! WHAT'RE YOU DOING IN MY ROOM AGAIN, YOU SNOOP?!
EVERYTHING I REALLY WANT IS ALWAYS WELL-HIDDEN IN YOUR ROOM. SO THERE MUST BE SOME LILIES OF THE VALLEY HERE!
W

CAZENOVE & WILLIAM

TAG!
YOU'RE IT!

?

HA HA HA

WHEN WE SAY A GAME'S OVER, IT...IS... O-V-E-R!

YOU'RE A SORE LOSER, ANYWAY!

BONK

BONK

CAZENOVE & WILLIAM

OOH, *RAPUNZEL*... YOUR HAIR'S AS BEAUTIFUL AS MY HORSE'S MANES.

TA-*DAAAH*, SUPER M...

YOU'RE SO SWEET, *FLYNN RIDER*...AND WHAT MUSCLES!

I'M SO IN LOVE WITH YOU.

KISS ME ON THE LIPS. YOU SMELL SO GOOD, ALMOST AS GOOD AS A JAR OF NULTELA.

UMM, YOU'RE DOING THE KISS WRONG, *LULU*.

FLYNN'S ARM SHOULDER HAS TO GO ONTO RAPUNZEL'S OTHER SHOULDER...

...THAT WAY SHE WON'T FALL BACKWARDS!

IT'S LIKE THIS ON TV, YOU SEE?!

WOOW!

IT DOESN'T WORK. LOOK, THEIR NOSES ARE TOUCHING!

WAIT...I'LL BE RIGHT BACK!

WENDY... WENDY...

WHEN YOU KISS *MASON* ON THE LIPS, WHERE DOES YOUR NOSE GO?

CAZENOVE & WILLIAM

9:00

9:30

BRUSH
BRUSH
BRUSH

10:00

10:30

11:00

11:30

12:00

I'M TELLING YOU IT'S NOT JUST A MIRROR. IT'S GOT TO BE A TV OR DVD PLAYER, TOO, I BET.

YEAH, WHICH EXPLAINS WHY MY SISTER SPENDS SO MANY HOURS IN FRONT OF IT!

CAZENOVE & WILLIAM

WHEN I CAME HOME FROM SCHOOL THIS AFTERNOON, I HAD A STRANGE SURPRISE...

HEYYY... HERE I AM...

I'M BACK FROM SCHOOL... I'M HUNGRY... I'M THIRSTY... OOOH, HEEEY...

NO ONE'S HERE TO WELCOME ME HOME? MY PARENTS DON'T HAVE SCHOOL!

UMM... MOM...WHY'RE YOU MEASURING MY BED? DID IT GROW, TOO?

WELL, YOU KNOW, SWEETHEART, IT'S BEEN A LONG TIME SINCE--

DON'T TELL ME YOU'RE GOING TO THROW IT OUT?!

MY BED HASN'T DONE ANYTHING TO YOU!

I'VE HAD IT SINCE I WAS LITTLE...

THE TWO OF US HAVE SO MANY MEMORIES TOGETHER!

OKAY, AS YOU WISH, MAUREEN.

WE WERE THINKING OF RE-DOING YOUR ROOM AND GETTING YOU A BIG BED. BUT IF YOU'D RATHER KEEP THIS ONE--

MAKE WAY... I'M BRINGING MY BOOKCASE AND MY DESK DOWN...COME ON, COME ON!

69

CAZENOVE x WILLIAM

MY NEW BED'S ANNOYING...

KREEE

CRACK

EEEKrr

IT NEVER STOPS MAKING NOISE...

CREEE

EEECRAKK

CROOOAHK

EEEK

MOM SAYS IT'S THE WOOD WORKING ITSELF OUT...

CREEE

EEEEKKK

CREEESS

AS IF THIS WAS THE RIGHT TIME FOR WORKING OUT, HONESTLY...

GRWL
CROOFEEK

WENDY, CAN I COME SLEEP WITH YOU? PRETTY PLEASE...?

MY BED WON'T STOP MAKING A BIG RACKET!

GNFR
FRGNN
GZZZ...

AT LEAST YOU DON'T HEAR WENDY'S BED...

SNORE ZZZ

BUT, I REALLY SHOULD THINK ABOUT EXCHANGING SISTERS!

SNOORE

SNOOOORE
OO

CAZENOVE & WILLIAM

WHEN WE PLAY TENNIS, *MAUREEN'S* ALWAYS A SMART ALECK. THAT *BUUUGS* ME!

HEH-HEH. MY TURN TO *SERVE!*

LOOK! I'VE GOT MY *GAME FACE* ON!

15 *LOVE!*

DON'T YOU JUST TOTALLY *LOVE* THIS GAME?

LOVE LOVE LOVE LOVE LOVE

AND THERE YOU GO--I'M OVER THE NET!

HA HA HA

WATCH OUT, *WENDY!* NO MORE *SKIRTING* BY!

FINE, STOP BEING A *DIMWIT.*

CAN WE FINISH PLAYING ALREADY?!

FINE. ⸲PFFF⸲ YOU DON'T GET *ANY* OF MY *JOKES!*

POCK

BUT TENNIS IS REALLY *BORING!* LET'S SWITCH IT UP AND PLAY...

...*POOL!* YELLOW BALL IN THE SIDE POCKET!

CAZENOVE & WILLIAM

I LOOOVE MY NEW BEDDD!

ZBOING

IT'S SOOOO GREAT!

I LOVE LIFE!

IT'S SUPER-MEGA BIG...

YAHOO!

IT'S THE BESTEST BED IN THE WORLD!

≥RRRAAAH≤....
WHAT'RE YOU DOING IN MY ROOM AGAIN?!

GET OUT... YOU'VE GOT 2 SECONDS TO CLEAR YOUR TOES OUT OF HERE!

YOU RODENT!

THE MARSUPA-MAUREEN IS GOING TO JUMP ON HER OWN BED LIKE A TRAMPOLINE!

WAIT, BUT MY BED'S BRAND NEW... I DON'T WANT TO WRECK IT BY JUMPING ON IT LIKE A MORON!

CAZENOVE & WILLIAM

I GOT IT!

I GOT IT!

MOM, IT'S FOR YOU.

AUNTIE COCO.

WENDY... FOR YOU...

...YOUR BOYFRIEND!

DADDY--

--YOUR EDITOR!

GRRR... WRONG NUMBER!

POOH — — THEY'RE WORTHLESS!

MAUREEEEN... TELEPHOOOOONE...

WOW, WHO COULD IT BE?

I'M SO HAPPY!

WELL, AREN'T YOU GOING TO PICK IT UP?

GET A MOVE ON, IN CASE IT TURNS OUT TO BE FOR ME!

BRIING-BRIING

73

CAZENOVE & WILLIAM

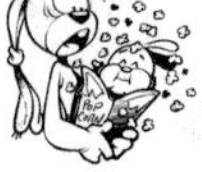

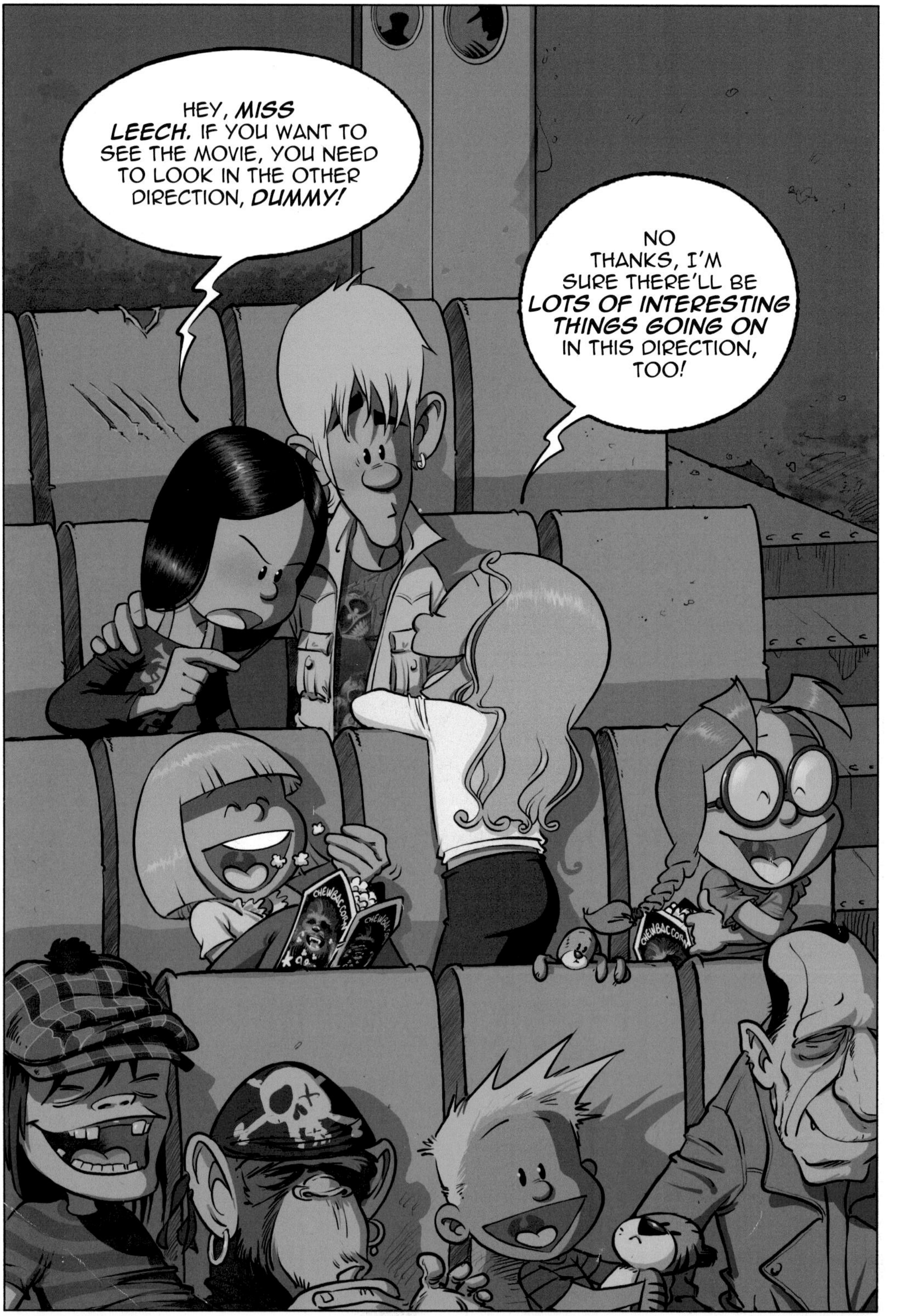
HEY, MISS LEECH. IF YOU WANT TO SEE THE MOVIE, YOU NEED TO LOOK IN THE OTHER DIRECTION, DUMMY!
NO THANKS, I'M SURE THERE'LL BE LOTS OF INTERESTING THINGS GOING ON IN THIS DIRECTION, TOO!

CAZENOVE & WILLIAM

YOO-HOO... DIDJA SEE, GIRLS?

OH, YEAH, SO CLASSY!

WOOOW! IT'S SO CUTE!

IT'S A *PANDA* UMBRELLA--MY FAVORITE ANIMAL IN MY WHOLE LIFE!

SWEET!

I AM SOOO JEALOUS.

PANDAS ARE SO SWEET, SO CUTE, SO NICE, AND ALL THAT.

I'M SO INTO THEM!

BUT I SAW ON TV THAT SOMETIMES THEY CAN BE VERY *AGGRESSIVE!*

YOUR TV'S *STUPID.*

ACTUALLY, WASN'T THAT ORIGINALLY YOUR SISTER'S UMBRELLA?!

YES, BUT SHE TOLD ME SHE'D GIVE IT TO ME.

IN YOUR DREAMS, HEDGEHOPPER! I'VE BEEN LOOKING FOR IT FOR AGES.

THAT ANIMAL'S *VERY* AGGRESSIVE. I WAS RIGHT!

I'M FED UP WITH YOU TAKING MY THINGS!

THUNK THUNK

OW! OW!

SPLISH   SPLASH

CAZENOVE & WILLIAM

I'M BORROWING A BUNCH OF YOUR STUFFED ANIMALS, WENDY!

THANKS!

OKAY, I GET IT...YOU'RE GETTING READY TO HAVE A GARAGE SALE, RIGHT?

NOT AT ALL! HANG ON, YOU CAN'T IMAGINE HOW MANY STUFFED ANIMALS IT TAKES TO COVER MY BIG NEW BED...

IT'S CRAZY!

CAZENOVE & WILLIAM

MAUREEN WAS A TOTAL PAIN AGAIN TODAY...

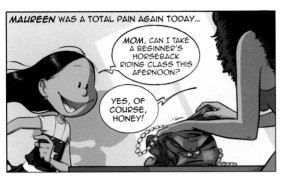

MOM, CAN I TAKE A BEGINNER'S HORSEBACK RIDING CLASS THIS AFERNOON?

YES, OF COURSE, HONEY!

WOOW! THAT'S 'ZACTLY WHAT I WAS GOING TO ASK TO DO, TOO!

YAHOO!

I ADORE HORSE FACT FINDING... I WANT TO GO! I WANT TO GO! I WANT TO GO!

ANYWAY, SO I HAD TO DRAG *MISS LEECH* ALONG WITH ME TO THE PONY CLUB...

EQUESTRIAN CENTER

GALLOPING TRAIL

STABLES

DO YOU THINK THIS IS IT, *WENDY?*

OF COURSE, SHE HAD TO HAVE THE SAME EQUIPMENT AS ME...

NOW WE'RE REAL KNIGHTS!

THE SAME KIND OF HORSE...

IS *THIS* MY TWIN PONY? WHERE'D THE SECOND ONE GO?

AND THE SAME COURSE... LITTLE MISS POT O' GLUE ALL THE WAY THROUGH...

EVERYONE INTO THEIR SADDLES FOR A LITTLE WALK THROUGH THE WOODS.

AND RIGHT WHEN WE LEFT FOR THE WALK...

NO MORE MAUREEN...SHE DISAPPEARED...!

SHE MUST'VE *SLIPPED* AWAY!

CAZENOVE & WILLIAM

BABY BABY
BABY OOH-HOO

⇒ACK!⇐
WAIT TWO
MINUTES, PRETTY
PLEASE...

...THERE'S SOME
THING-A-MA-JIGGY IN
THESE SKATES THAT'S
BUGGING ME AND GIVING
ME *HORROR-HIVES*
TO ROLLERBLADE...

OKAY, OKAY,
BUT STEP
ON IT!

BUGS ME

BUUUUGGGGSSSS ME.
⇒AAARRRRGGGGH⇐...

I'M THE
ONE YOU'RE
BUGGING WITH
ALL THIS WAITING!
ARE YOU GOING
TO BE DONE
SOON?!

I'M A BIG GIRL
NOW, I DON'T
NEED TRAINING
WHEELS ANY
LONGER...

...THEY MADE
ME FALL MORE
THAN ANYTHING
ELSE!

CLACK

CLACK

78

CAZENOVE & WILLIAM

≥AHEM≥...

MAKING A DRESS OUT OF THE LIVING ROOM CURTAINS...?

I ALREADY DID THAT WHEN I WAS 6 YEARS OLD!

MAKING COOTIE CATCHERS FROM *DAD'S* COMIC STRIPS?

I DID THAT, TOO!

PAINT USING *MOM'S* FOUNDATION...

...ONE OF MY GREAT CLASSICS!

SHAVING THE SOFA...

I USED TO DO THAT AT LEAST ONCE A YEAR!

I'VE GOT TONS MORE I CAN TELL YOU ABOUT, IF YOU WANT.

SEE YOU LATER.

TONS?

HI, *MOM,* I HAD A BIG LIST OF BAD THINGS TO DO...

IF YOU COULD CROSS OUT THE ONES THAT *WENDY'S* ALREADY DONE, THAT WOULD SAVE ME SOME TIME.

CAZENOVE & WILLIAM

TELL ME, *WENDY*, DO YOU THINK THE MOON COULD KISS THE SUN?

≵PFFF≵... YOU *ALWAYS* HAVE TO BABBLE ON.

NO, BUT SERIOUSLY. IT COULD DO IT WHEN THERE'S AN ECLIPSE, DON'T YOU THINK?

WHATEVS!

OR MAYBE... IT'S MAD AT THE SUN.

THAT'S WHY IT'S GOT A PALE-FACED COMPLEXION. IT'S A BIG GLOOMY GUS!

HEY, THERE'S YOUR *MASON* COMING BACK FROM THE FESTIVAL...

UH... HE'S HOLDING *SAMMIE'S* HAND... IS THAT OKAY?

BOO-HOO-HOO-HOO-HOOoo...

COME ON, DON'T CRY.. YOU KNOW...

...MAYBE THE MOON JUST DOESN'T HAVE A *SISTER* TO COMFORT HER.

80

CAZENOVE & WILLIAM

HEY, *MAUREEN*, WHAT DO YOU THINK ABOUT US SPENDING THE DAY TOGETHER?

NOTHING BUT YOU AND ME.

REALLY? YOU AREN'T KIDDING?

WELL, NO! ARE WE SISTERS OR NOT?

IT'S SO STRANGE...EVER SINCE *WENDY'S* NO LONGER BEEN WITH *MASON*, SHE'S BEEN SUPER CLOSE TO ME...

DO YOU WANT MY POPCORN?

THIS FILM'S SO GOOD, DON'T YOU THINK?

SHHHH...

STRAWBERRY AND LEMON, MY FAVORITE FLAVORS.

MINE TOO. I LOVE THOSE THE BEST!

WE'VE TOLD EACH OTHER LOTS OF SECRETS AND ALL...

HA-HA-HA. YOU SHOULD'VE SEEN THE LOOK ON *AUDREY'S* FACE!

LOL!

BWAHAHA... TEE-HEE-HEE-HEE

KEEP FF THE RASS

...I ALMOST FELT AS IF I WAS PLAYING THE PART THAT MASON USED TO PLAY...

WHAT'LL WE DO NOW, WENDY?

LET'S GO SIT ON THE BENCH AGAIN.

MASON'S PART...

OKAY! BUT YOU'D BETTER NOT TRY TO GIVE ME AN *ICKY FRENCH KISS*, I'M WARNING YOU!

KEEP OFF THE GRASS

CAZENOVE & WILLIAM

WHAT'S GOTTEN INTO HER AGAIN **THIS** TIME?

SHE SPENT HER WEDNESDAY MORNING RUMMAGING THROUGH MY THINGS, NO DOUBT...

...OR SHE NICKED MY PERFUME, MY DEODORANT, MY HAIR CLIPS, OR MY NAIL POLISH, I BET.

NO, SHE DIDN'T EVEN TOUCH MY DIARY... EVERYTHING'S WHERE IT BELONGS!

HEY, YOU! HALF-PINT! WERE YOU LOOKING FOR ME?

WHO, ME?

YES, **YOU**... WHAT WERE YOU DOING IN MY ROOM, EH? DID YOU DO SOMETHING BAD AGAIN?! COME ON, FESS UP!

AH, NO, I DIDN'T DO ANYTHING, CROSS MY HEART AND HOPE TO DIE!

I'M JUST PRACTICING CLEARING OUT AT FULL SPEED WHEN I REALLY DO.

CAZENOVE & WILLIAM

WENDY, YOO-HOO...

...I'VE GOT SOME TOTALLY TERRIFIC NEWS...

IF YOU NEED A MASSAGE, I'M A SUPER-PRO.

AND LOOK... I MADE A PRICE LIST. IT'S CHEAP!

NOT INTERESTED.

BUT LOOK!

5 DOLLARS FOR A FOOT MASSAGE. 3 DOLLARS FOR A BACK MASSAGE. 2 DOLLARS FOR A LEG.

Massage
FUT 5.-
BAK 3
LEK 1
ELBOS 0
NEES ...... -

ELBOWS AND KNEES ARE *FREE!*

I'M BUSY HERE, IN CASE YOU DIDN'T NOTICE.

SHOO! SCRAM!

LET ME SHOW YOU... I'VE BEEN PRACTICING ON *MR. BUN BUN* AND HE TOLD ME I WAS REALLY GIFTED.

WHAT SHOULD I START WITH?

ARGH!

I DON'T BELIEVE IT!

MY BACK'S FINE-- LEAVE ME ALONE AND GO JUMP OFF A CLIFF!

HERE YOU GO!

YOU'LL *LOVE* IT!

CRACK

UH... HEE-HEE... NO CHARGE FOR YOUR FIRST SESSION, OF COURSE.

-GRRRR...

83

CAZENOVE & WILLIAM

LULU'S GOING TO HAVE A MEGA-BASH TONIGHT...

YAA-HOOOO!

I HAVE TO PRACTICE... I'VE PREPARED LOTS OF MEGA-TOP CDs!

MY GARBAGE BAG DANCE...

IT ROCKS!

STAIRWAY DANCE...

...SO AMAZING!

GARDEN HOSE DANCE...

DISHWASHING DANCE...

THAT EVENING...

SO, MAUREEN, YOU DON'T DANCE?

YES, BUT YOU WOULDN'T HAPPEN TO HAVE A GARBAGE CAN OR A STAIRWAY?

OR EVEN SOME DISHES TO WASH?

CAZENOVE & WILLIAM

YOU SHOULD BE SORRY, *MASON*...YOU STILL WENT OUT WITH MY BEST FRIEND...

UH-OH... SOMEONE'S IN *HOT WATER!*

BUT I CAN EXPLAIN, *WENDY.* ACTUALLY, I DIDN'T GO OUT WITH--

WELL, YES, BUT NO...

...SHE WAS ALREADY THERE AND... SINCE I WAS THERE, TOO... WELL, I, WE, US...

...I SWEAR I JUST WALKED HER HOME, SEE?!

YOU'RE THE ONE I LIKE, WENDY. I DON'T LIKE HER AT ALL, I SWEAR TO YOU...

WELL, OKAY, SHE'S NICE, TOO, BUT... NOT LIKE YOU ARE, Y'KNOW... I...

UM, DO YOU WANT SOMETHING TO DRINK, WENDY?

I...I'LL BE RIGHT BACK.

OOPS! HE'S HEADED THIS WAY!

WERE YOU LISTENING TO WHAT I WAS SAYING TO YOUR SISTER?!

HUH? WHAT SISTER?!

DO YOU WANT ME TO GIVE YOU A HAND WITH YOUR HOMEWORK?

NO, I'M FINE. BESIDES, YOU'RE WORTHLESS AT *EXPLANATIONING* ANYWAY!

85

CAZENOVE & WILLIAM

MAUREEN FINALLY DECIDED TO GO CLIMBING...

...AND CHOSE INDOOR BOULDERING...

SOMETHING FOR PROS, EH...

CLIPS

CLOPS

HEY! THAT'S MAUREEN OVER THERE!

YOO-HOO, MAAUREEENN!

BEEP BEEP

WERE YOU IN THE FENCING CLASS? I DIDN'T SEE YOU

ROCK CLIMBING!

WOW! ROCK CLIMBING MUST BE GREAT!

≥PFFFF≤ I HATE IT.

BUT, WHY THE--

MAUREEEEEN!

YOU BUSTED UP MY NINTENDOX AGAIN!

AH, OKAY... NOW I UNDERSTAND WHY YOU'RE ROCK CLIMBING...

YUP! IT'S A QUESTION OF SURVIVAL!

≥GRRRR≤...

CAZENOVE x WILLIAM

STRANGE DAY TODAY...

FIRST, **MASON** CAME TO APOLOGIZE TO **WENDY** FOR GOING OUT WITH **SAMMIE**...

BOO-HOO-HOO-HOO-HOOoo...

AFTER THAT, SAMMIE CAME TO ASK WENDY'S FORGIVENESS FOR STEALING HER BOYFRIEND...

SORRY-SORRY-SORRY...

SHE ALSO APOLOGIZED TO MASON...

YOU'RE SO GOOD TOGETHER...

AND AFTER THAT, WENDY ASKED SAMMIE AND MASON TO FORGIVE HER FOR SULKING...

I LOVE YOU BOTH!

≠TSSSK≠...YOU THREE REALLY ARE *IDIOTS*!

YOU'RE ALL PATHETIC.

WHY ON EARTH ARE YOU BEING SO MEAN, *MAUREEN*? WHY'D YOU SAY THAT?

JUST SO I COULD APOLOGIZE, TOO...

...I REALLY LOVE HUGS!

CAZENOVE & WILLIAM

MAUREEN'S TRIED EVERYTHING...

IF I WIN THE MATCH, YOU'LL GIVE ME MY BIRTHDAY PRESENT, OKAY?

NO WORRIES!

IF I GET THERE FIRST, CAN I HAVE IT?

DON'T WORRY...

WILL I GET MY PRESENT IF I GET A KING?

DON'T WORRY...

IF YOU MAKE FEWER BOUNCES THAN ME, I GET MY PRESENT!

YES!

THAT'S THREE ALREADY!

IF I BOUNCE HIGHER THAN YOU EVEN ONCE...

- LOL!

...I'LL GET MY PRESENT?!

...AND IT'S BEEN LIKE THAT EVERY DAY SINCE HER BIRTHDAY!

BUT THAT WAS THREE MONTHS AGO ALREADY?!

YOU'RE TAKING ADVANTAGE OF HER, WENDY!

SHE'S THE ONE WHO CARES ABOUT GETTING IT BY BEATING ME AT SOMETHING...

...BUT I THINK SHE'S GOING TO LET HERSELF GET IT NOW.

IF I'M SMALLER THAN YOU, I'LL GET MY PRESENT NOW?!

CAZENOVE & WILLIAM

I HOPE YOU'RE READY, MAUREEN?

SUPER-READY!

THEN YOU'VE GOT 3 MINUTES TO FIND YOUR PRESENT!

3...2...1... GO!

TAP

I'M GOING TO FIND IT!

I'M GOING TO FIND IT!

I'M GOING TO FIND IT!

I'M GOING TO FIND IT!

I'M GOING TO FIND IT!

WOOOW! BUT SHE'S DESTROYING YOUR ROOM NOW!

YUP! LOL! IT'S SO CRAZY TO WATCH HER TAKE MY ROOM APART.

AND IF SHE FINDS HER PRESENT?

NO CHANCE... I'VE GOT IT ON ME!

GO ON, YOU'VE STILL GOT A MINUTE-AND-A-HALF TO HANG ON.

I'M GOING TO FIND IT!

YAY!

I'M GOING TO FIND IT!

STOP THAT STOPWATCH FOR ME!

CAZENOVE & WILLIAM

I LOVE GIVING *BIG HUGS*...

SURPRISE HUGS FOR *MOM* AND *DAD*, OF COURSE...

>RAAAH< BUT-- >AARGH<

...AND ALWAYS TO MY BEST BUDS...

UHM...THE TEACHER'S LOOKING AT US, *MAUREEN*...

...TO MY BUDS' BOYFRIEND...

I SWEAR I'VE GOT NOTHING TO DO WITH IT. SHE'S THE ONE WHO--

...TO MY SISTER'S BUDS...

WHOA, THERE! THIS IS GETTING *STRANGE*...

WITH *WENDY*, I HAVE TO BE CUNNING. SHE ISN'T ALSWAY OKAY WITH BIG HUGS...

THE MAIL'S HERE...

OOOH... A TEEN MAG...

AND SINCE SHE CAN'T STAND FOR ME TO READ IT FIRST...

DON'T TOUCH MY MAGAZINE!

AND THERE IT IS--A BIG HUG ANYWAY!

CAZENOVE & WILLIAM

SPECIALTY OF **CHEF MAUREEN:** "SUPER DELICIOUS COOKIES!"

THEY'LL MAKE YOU FORGET **MASON**, YOU'LL SEE...

MMM, THANKS.

THERE'S LOTS OF THINGS IN 'EM. YOU'RE **SOOO** GOING TO LOVE 'EM.

OH, GEEZ. IT TASTES LIKE FEET.

YUCK!

THEY'VE GOT CHOCOLATE, BRIE, AND LETTUCE FOR COLOR...

I'LL BRING OUT THE NEXT ONE.

TA-DAAAH!

TOMATO CAKES. I KNOW YOU LOVE THEM BUT I DIDN'T BAKE IT 'CUZ I PREFER RAW DOUGH...

HOW ABOUT **A HOUSE COCKTAIL** TO HELP EVERYTHING GO DOWN...

I PUT IN EVERYTHING I FOUND IN THE FRIDGE-- APPLES, ZUCCHINI, CAULIFLOWER...

TOMORROW, I'LL MAKE YOU A **FLOWER PIE...**

...I FOUND THE RECIPE IN A COMIC-BOOK.

UGH!

REALLY, **WENDY?** YOU'D LIKE TO GO OUT WITH ME AGAIN, TOMORROW?

WELL, YES, I'D LIKE TO VERY MUCH...

...MY STOMACH'S COUNTING ON IT!

91

CAZENOVE & WILLIAM

HEY, *WENDY*, DO YOU REMEMBER HOW I STUCK TO YOU WHEN WE WERE LITTLE...

...WORSE THAN A PIECE OF CHEWING GUM ON THE BOTTOM OF A SNEAKER?

I'D SAY A *LEECH*, INSTEAD.

REMEMBER WHEN I USED TO HIDE MYSELF BEHIND A BUSH TO WATCH YOU FLIRT?

AND YOU THOUGHT WE DIDN'T SEE YOU, ⸬*TSSSK*⸬...

SLICE SLICE

BANG

AND WHEN I USED TO WORM MY WAY BETWEEN THE TWO OF YOU AT THE MOVIES...

LOL, YOU'D MAKE ONE OF THOSE FACES EVERY TIME!

AND YOU WOULD SAY IT WAS JUST TO KEEP FROM GETTING COLD.

ONE TIME I EVEN I HID A WALKIE-TALKIE UNDER YOUR PILLOW...

...SO I COULD HEAR EVERYTHING YOU BABBLED TO YOUR BOYFRIEND ON THE PHONE.

HA! YOUR WALKIE-TALKIE WOUND UP IN THE GARBAGE CAN!

HEE-HEE... WHEN I THINK ABOUT IT, I WAS PRETTY CLOSE TO BEING A *PEST*, A *LEECH*, A *SNOOP*, A *GATECRASHER*...

ANYWAY, ARE YOU HAVING SOMETHING GOOD TO EAT WITH *MASON*? I'M ABSOLUTELY STARVING!

⸬*MMPH*⸬...

IT'S A CURSE. WE'LL *NEVER, EVER* BE ALONE--JUST THE TWO OF US!

CAZENOVE & WILLIAM

WATCH OUT FOR PAPERCUTZ ™

Welcome to the thrilling third THE SISTERS graphic novel, featuring those testy tween(ish) terrors, Wendy and Maureen, by Christophe Cazenove and William Maury, from Papercutz—that pseudo dysfunctional faux-family dedicated to publishing great graphic novels for all ages. I'm Jim Salicrup, the Editor-in-Chief and Honorary Third Sister, and I'm here to take you behind-the-scenes at Papercutz and tell you about our most exciting new project…

Papercutz is launching not just one all-new graphic novel series, not just two all-new graphic novel series, but an entire new <u>line</u> of graphic novels created just for you! That is if you're interested in graphic novels featuring great characters, in amazing situations, having awesome adventures, with a touch of romance. If so, Charmz is just what you've been looking for! Charmz, the all-new imprint from Papercutz. And here's a list of the first few Charmz graphic novels…

STITCHED Copyright © 2017 Mariah McCourt and Aaron Alexovich.

First up is STITCHED, by Mariah McCourt, writer (and Charmz Editor), and Aaron Alexovich, artist. STITCHED is a supernatural tale about Crimson Volania Mulch, a rag-doll girl who wakes up in a cemetery, but doesn't know anything except her name. Her first few nights "alive" are a spooky whirlwind of ghosts, werewolves, witches, and weirdly-beautiful boys. Will she find out where she comes from? Do two-headed badger/hedgehogs eat cupcakes? Does Crimson even have time for romance when she doesn't even know who she is? Or does she have to fall apart before she can be whole again?

Next there's SWEETIES, based on Cathy Cassidy's novel *The Chocolate Box Girls*, adapted by Véronique Grisseaux, writer, and Anna Merli, artist. SWEETIES is about blending two families into one. Cherry acquires four half-sisters, Honey, Skye, Summer, and Coco, when her candy-making father Paddy marries their mother, Charlotte. Things get complicated when Cherry falls for Honey's boyfriend and Skye falls in love with the man of her dreams – literally!

Les Filles au Chocolat [SWEETIES] Copyright © 2014, 2015, 2017 Jungle! The Chocolate Box Girls © 2010, 2011, 2017 by Cathy Cassidy.

Finally (for now) there's CHLOE, by Greg Tessier, writer, and Amandine, co-writer and artist. Chloe Blin is determined to be popular, confident, and in love! Unfortunately she has to deal with mean girl cliques, fashion faux pas, and trying to impress the cutest boy in school with her sweet moves… only to fall completely flat. Whether it's rocking a party that goes sideways or making the best of a less than ideal vacation, Chloe may not always get it right at first, but she doesn't give up!

Charmz editor Mariah McCourt wants these graphic novels to be "the book equivalent of a hot chocolate; sweet, maybe a little dark sometimes, comforting, and made just for you. You can curl up with our tales, settle in, and enjoy falling in love with our characters just like they fall in love with each other."

To get a better idea what these graphic novels are like, check out the special preview pages of STITCHED, SWEETIES, and CHLOE on the following pages. The graphic novels are available now at booksellers and libraries everywhere.

For more information, and more sneak previews of Charmz titles, and all the latest Papercutz news, be sure to visit us at papercutz.com. And don't forget to contact us an let us know what you think of everything we're up to! We also suspect you won't want to miss THE SISTERS #4 "Selfie-Awareness," coming soon to those very same wonderful booksellers and libraries!

Thanks,

Jim

Mistinguette [CHLOE] Copyright © 2011, 2012, 2017 Jungle!

STAY IN TOUCH!

EMAIL: salicrup@papercutz.com
WEB: www.papercutz.com
TWITTER: @papercutzgn
INSTAGRAM: @papercutzgn
FACEBOOK: PAPERCUTZGRAPHICNOVELS
REGULAR MAIL: Papercutz, 160 Broadway, Suite 700, East Wing, New York, NY 10038

Special Preview of STITCHED Available Now at Booksellers Everywhere!

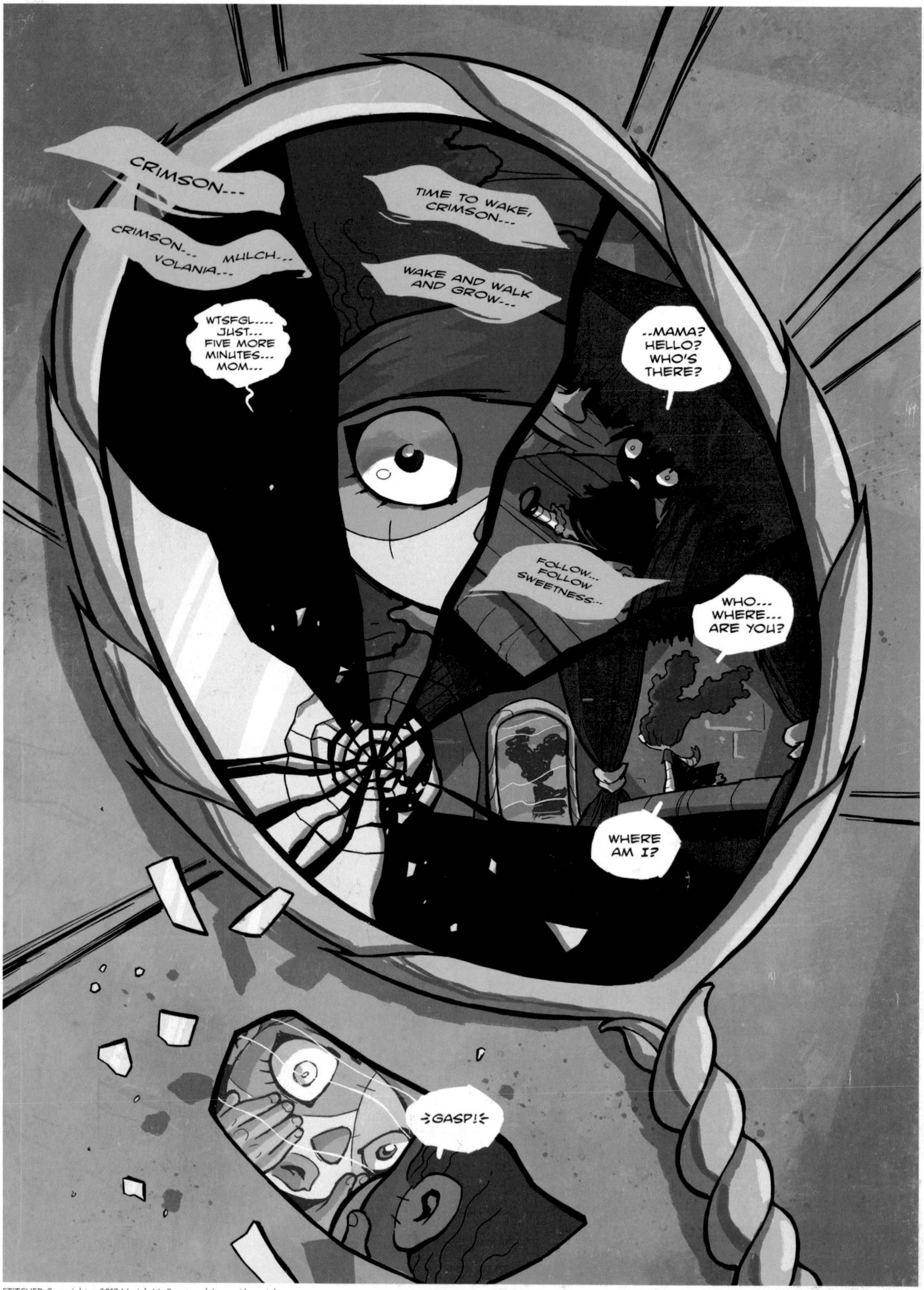
CRIMSON...
CRIMSON... MULCH... VOLANIA...
TIME TO WAKE, CRIMSON...
WAKE AND WALK AND GROW...
WTSFGL.... JUST... FIVE MORE MINUTES... MOM...
..MAMA? HELLO? WHO'S THERE?
FOLLOW... FOLLOW SWEETNESS...
WHO... WHERE... ARE YOU?
WHERE AM I?
GASP!

GLASGOW, SCOTLAND. CLYDE ACADEMY.

CAN'T LIE.

THERE ARE SOME THINGS I'LL MISS ABOUT CLYDE ACADEMY.

LIKE THIS *DELIGHTFUL* LUNCH FOOD.

OR STARING AT THE BACK OF RYAN CLEGG'S... NECK.

THERE ARE ALSO THINGS I WILL *NOT* MISS:

LIKE MATH TESTS AND--

KIRSTY McRAE!

SHE AND HER FRIENDS DRIVE ME CRAZY!

EXCUSE ME, CHERRY COSTELLO!

WE NEED SOME MORE ROOM.

WAP

HEY, GIRLS!

DID YOU KNOW, CHERRY'S MUM THOUGHT SHE WAS SUCH A *LOSER* THAT SHE DITCHED HER AND RAN OFF TO LIVE ON THE OTHER SIDE OF THE WORLD?

YOU DON'T KNOW ANYTHING ABOUT MY MUM!

An evening before school starts up, in an ordinary, small town.

IT'S HARD TO BE THE NEW GIRL.

I HOPE I CAN MAKE MYSELF SOME NEW, COOL, FRIENDS. RIGHT, CARTOON?

IT'S TIME TO GO TO BED!

QUIET *DOWN*, I KNOW WHAT TIME IT IS! DON'T COME IN MY ROOM!

I WILL IF I WANNA!

IF I WANNA!

IF I WANNA!

STOP!

CALM DOWN IN HERE! ARTHUR, LEAVE YOUR SISTER CHLOE ALONE. SHE'S GOT ENOUGH STRESS WITHOUT YOU ADDING TO IT!

COME ON OUT AND NO ARGUING!

SWEET DREAMS, LITTLE MISTY!

GOOD-NIGHT, MOM.